2 0 9 9
firestorm

2099

firestorm

John Peel

BOOK 6

AN
APPLE
PAPERBACK

SCHOLASTIC INC.
New York Toronto London Auckland Sydney
Mexico City New Delhi Hong Kong

ISBN 0-439-06035-4

12 11 10 9 8 7 6 5 4 3 2 1   0 1 2 3 4 5 6/0

Printed in the U.S.A.

First Scholastic printing, July 2000

*This is for David Levithan
once again, for everything.*

2 0 9 9

firestorm

Prologue

Kevan Moss had always loved living on the Moon. His parents were two of the original colonists in Armstrong City, and Moss had been born there. He had never thought he'd regret it.

Until today.

A cold hand of fear had clamped around his chest, making breathing difficult. He was staring at the control panel for one of the fusion reactors that powered this section of the city.

Even though he was acting governor, it was no longer under his control.

"What is happening to it?" he asked the head technician. He couldn't remember the man's name, and right now it didn't seem to be important.

"It's been bypassed," the man answered. "Someone else has a program running. The mix is being altered slowly, causing the core temperature to rise. It isn't immediately dangerous, but the imbalance is increasing."

"How long do we have before . . . ?" Moss couldn't bring himself to finish the question, but that wasn't really necessary.

"They will all explode in about ten hours," the man said.

"Can't you do *anything*?" Moss demanded. That was what the man was paid for. Couldn't he do his job?

The technician shook his head. "That's a highly sophisticated program. Oh, I'm sure I could hack into it, given enough time. But it would take me at least a day, and one mistake on my part would engage a secondary subroutine that would simply dump the fuel into the mix immediately. There'd be a premature detonation." He shrugged. "Instead of waiting to die, we'd all be vaporized. I *know* I don't have the skill to beat this program, and I don't believe anyone else on the Moon has, either. The only thing I can suggest is complete evacuation of all cities, while we still have time."

"We may have the time," Moss said bitterly, "but we don't have the ability. The same maniac who did this" —

he gestured at the control panel — "also wrecked the docking ports. We can't get any ships down here to evacuate people." Moss had spoken to the boy behind this — a fourteen-year-old genius named Devon. The boy simply wanted everyone to die, and it looked as if he was going to achieve his goal. "Nor can we bring in any help. It'll take more than a day to clear any of the ports for action again."

Now the technician was looking very gray, as the desperation of their situation sank in. "Can't we get help from Earth?" he asked. "Surely there's somebody in Computer Control who can break this program. Can't someone there help us?"

"I don't know," Moss answered. "I've been trying to contact them, but they have some kind of emergency of their own right now. I have to wait for them to get back to me."

"Wait?" The man was almost hysterical. "How long can we wait?"

"No longer than ten hours," Moss replied, staring at the panels. They showed a small but significant temperature rise already. As time went on, it would get worse.

"What are we going to tell people?" the man wanted to know.

"What *can* we tell them?" Moss grimaced. "That

we're sorry, but they've got ten hours left of their lives?" He shook his head. "That would only create panic, and wouldn't help anyone. Right now, only you, your immediate staff, and I know about this. And that's how it's going to stay."

The man stared at him in horror. "Don't you think people have a right to know they're going to die?"

Moss sighed. "If we make an announcement, it will only cause the same shock and horror in them as it has in us. We'd have a mob on our hands, demanding action, trying to flee the city. On foot!"

"Maybe we should give them the chance."

"What chance?" Moss gestured at the reactor. "When that blows, all power on the Moon will be gone. Anybody who gets out on foot would only live as long as their space suits can hold air. Then they'd slowly suffocate out on the surface. And that's assuming they can get far enough away from Armstrong to avoid the blast. They're going to die, and I think they'd be better doing it in a microsecond than gasping to death over several hours, don't you?"

"Who gave you the right to make that decision for them?" the man asked bitterly.

"Nobody," Moss admitted. "But somebody has to do it, and right now I'm in charge. So it's my call."

Moss turned his back on the man and walked slowly

out of the room. He'd never wanted to be in charge here; he liked being an assistant to the governor. But he'd been thrust into power because the governor was in jail, awaiting trial. It looked like he'd never get his day in any lunar court. And Moss was having to make decisions that meant life — or, in this case, death — for every man, woman, and child on the Moon.

He wanted to scream.

1

"**W**ell?" asked Taki Shimoda of the room at large. "What are we going to do?" There was no immediate answer from any of the ashen faces staring back at her around the conference table. It was hard to believe that she was in the company of the most powerful people in the entire world. But it wasn't at all hard to believe that they were as scared as she was, and as powerless at this moment.

Computer Control ran EarthNet, the vast electronic web that linked together almost every human being on Earth. It controlled everything, from flitters for transport to the pedways, aircraft and spaceship launches to submarine cruisers, hospitals to fire stations, farms to shopping. If anything happened to EarthNet, the whole of human life on Earth would collapse.

Twice already, they had narrowly averted such a collapse. The attack on EarthNet had been coordinated by a group of renegades calling themselves Quietus. Thanks to a trap Shimoda had sprung, five members of Computer Control had been proven to be a part of the conspiracy. These included the president, Elinor Morgenstein, and Vice President Martin van Dreelen. The five had fled, escaping the trap cunningly. Now all Shimoda knew was that they were on their way to Mars. She didn't know where exactly they were, or on which ship they traveled. Unless she could discover this, the five of them would reach a safe haven on Mars.

Mars was going through its own terrible problems. Quietus had long planned to use it as a base for their activities, and the current Administrator was one of their agents. He had brought in shields from Earth who were loyal to Quietus, and with them had seized military control of Mars. A small band of rebels was fighting to secure their freedom, but there was little real news about what was happening. Shimoda knew that Computer Control couldn't allow this takeover to succeed, but there wasn't much that they could do to stop the Administrator.

Besides, they had a worse and more immediate problem to deal with.

Devon, the fourteen-year-old computer genius who had designed the Doomsday Virus, was back again. The virus was gone — at least for now — but the insane youth still aimed to become ruler of Earth. He had a new plan this time, one that left Computer Control with a terrible choice: hand complete power over EarthNet to Devon, or see the death of every living thing on the planet.

Luther Schein, head of Customer Relations, shifted uneasily in his seat. "What *can* we do?" he asked. "Are we sure that this Devon will carry out his plans? Destroying all life on Earth is . . . well, so crazy and extreme. And how do we know that he's telling the truth when he says he can do it?"

"He's deadly serious," Shimoda replied. "He's tried to destroy EarthNet twice already with the Doomsday Virus. We're simply very fortunate that it didn't work. I don't find it at all hard to believe that he means what he says. The boy has a fixation on power. As to whether it's possible . . ." She turned to Therese Copin. "You're head of Technology, and probably the best one to judge the matter. What do *you* think?"

Copin squirmed slightly. "He claims he's reprogrammed a waste freighter to come to Earth instead of orbiting, and that he has a bomb on board that he can trigger to rip the ship apart." She shrugged. "Both are simple enough to do, given that he's a hacking genius. I checked the lunar docking schedules, and there was a robot freighter that took off from the Moon at the time he said. I can't guarantee that he performed the sabotage, but it's certainly possible."

"Can't we check it out fairly simply?" asked Dennis Borden. The ninety-odd-year-old man looked like he was over a hundred from the strain. "Call up the flight records and transponder data."

Copin spread her hands. "I wish I could, but I can't get access to the ship. Something's taken it off-line. And I suspect that *something* is Devon."

Badni Jada, the head of Personnel, leaned forward. "I don't see the problem. Why don't we simply unpack one of the old nuclear missiles we've got in storage and shoot the ship down while it's still in space? Surely we've got the time for that?"

"The time, yes," Copin agreed. "Even though they're all locked away, we could have one ready for launch in eight hours. The problem is finding a target. We can't track the ship if the transponder isn't working."

"What about radar?" Anita Horesh, head of Development, asked. "It's got to show up on that."

"It doesn't," Copin countered. "Radar evasion technology these days is very sophisticated. Besides which, the radar grid from Overlook space station isn't working, thanks to Quietus's sabotage, so we don't have complete coverage. By the time we get a definite fix on the ship and can confirm it's the right one, it'll already be inside Earth's atmosphere."

"And if Devon *does* trigger his bomb," Borden asked her, "will it do what he says?"

"Yes." Copin was shaking, and Shimoda couldn't blame her. "The ship will rip apart, and all of the radioactive waste will spew out into the upper atmosphere. The jet streams will carry the dust all over Earth. It will fall to the ground and kill everything it touches. Every person, every plant, even every bacterium will die. This isn't like one of the Clouds, where it's a small contagion that can be tracked, and we can warn people until it dissipates. This will be *everywhere*. If Devon carries out his threat, then there will be no life on Earth at all within a week. And for hundreds of years, nothing will be able to live here until the radioactivity dies down. We're not talking about the end of the human race — the lunar cities, Mars, and Overlook will all be able to go on. But the vast majority of the human race — about ninety-five percent of it — will be annihilated."

"And you're saying that there's nothing directly we can do to stop it?" Shimoda asked.

"Not exactly." Copin hesitated. "But I *am* saying that I can't think of a way. If there is one, it'll take a better brain than mine to come up with it."

"Which leaves us one possible solution, then," Borden summarized. "We can give in to Devon's demands, and turn the Omega Circuit over to him."

Shimoda hated the thought of that. She'd only just learned what the Omega Circuit was — complete control over all of EarthNet by a single individual. Nobody would be able to override him, or remove him. And if anything happened to him, EarthNet would die along with him. This was what Devon wanted.

"I don't like that," she said firmly, and all eyes turned toward her. "For one thing, this boy is *insane*. Does any of us have any idea what he'd use that power for? Given what we've seen of him so far, I'd say it would be to torture and kill people."

"Isn't it better that a few suffer for the rest of us to live?" asked Jada.

"What if *you* are one of the ones picked to suffer?" Shimoda replied. "Would you still feel that way then?"

"Of course." Jada's eyes narrowed. "Better that I suffer than all life be wiped out."

"But it's not that simple," Shimoda argued. "If he gets the Omega Circuit, then it lasts only as long as he does. And I'm willing to bet that he has absolutely no in-

11

terest in transferring the power. He'll let it die with him. He's like a ruler of old, wanting to take his loyal subjects into death alongside him. Why let him torture Earth before he destroys it? Giving him the Omega Circuit will only delay the end, not stop it."

"You think he's that insane?" asked Miriam Rodriguez, head of Programming.

"I'm sure of it." Shimoda had no doubt in her mind. Devon's behavioral pattern so far virtually guaranteed it. "So the question is, do we buy the human race maybe a hundred more years at the expense of giving it over to Devon so he can torture, humiliate, and kill at will?"

"I take it you'd vote no," Borden said dryly.

Shimoda swallowed, remembering that she was talking about the death of the human race. "Better death than that," she replied. "I vote no."

"Anyone else have anything to say before we take a vote on the issue?"

"Yes," said a very unexpected voice from the doorway. Shimoda whirled around to see the last person she would have expected to see standing there.

The world really *had* gone mad.

2

On the spaceship *Santa Fe*, Elinor Morgenstein looked around the meeting room with a scowl on her face. Ben Quan, once head of Finance for Computer Control; Vladek Cominsky, former head of Planning; and the two senior vice presidents, Anna Fried and Martin Van Dreelen, all looked back. They were the heads of Quietus, and this was the first time that they had ever met as such. Even she, the founder of Quietus, hadn't known which of her colleagues was a part of her group. Secrecy had been essential, to prevent capture or betrayal.

"I have to first inform you all that the Malefactor will

not be joining us," she said. "It seems that he's been . . . detained by the authorities, and was unable to escape Earth before the Doomsday Virus was released. Meanwhile, it seems that we were quite correct in believing that Shimoda would track us down on Overlook. Thankfully, she fell for our decoy ship, and did not discover the *Santa Fe*. She is undoubtedly cursing us now, and will do so until EarthNet collapses. Then she'll have more important things to worry about."

"This all seems like excellent news to me," Cominsky said. "Why, then, the long face?"

"Because I've been monitoring EarthNet, and it has not collapsed yet. I can't hook in directly, of course, or the virus will spread to this ship and kill us all. But I've had scanners checking activity on Earth, and there is no sign of collapse yet. Why not?"

Quan shrugged. "Perhaps the Malefactor delayed the release of the virus for a while?" he suggested.

"He assured me that it had been done," Morgenstein snapped. "In which case, EarthNet *should* be destroyed. And it isn't yet."

"Perhaps," Van Dreelen suggested lazily, "Computer Control has managed to hold the virus off for a while. If you recall, Tristan Connor evolved some stealth dog programs that delayed the virus on its first release. The boy is still at large, and he may have done the same thing again. Not that he can hold off the virus. Just slow it down."

Morgenstein was relieved. "That has to be the answer," she agreed. "It merely delays the inevitable, then. But I still have to reprimand you, Van Dreelen. Why did you appoint this Shimoda as head of Security? She's proven to be a dangerous woman."

Van Dreelen spread his arms. "How was I to know that? I removed Chen, to nullify him, and I felt sure that promoting such a charming young woman would cause problems of resentment in the department and result in setbacks in Security. People were bound to suspect me of ulterior motives — which I confirmed by pestering her for dinner dates. I'm certain that everyone in Security thought I was giving her the job as a bribe. It did cause the problems I wanted, but there was an unexpected side effect. Shimoda turned out to be very, very good at what she does. We all saw Chen's report on how she messed up the investigation into the Doomsday Virus and went after the wrong suspect. I seem to remember everyone agreeing she was the perfect choice for head of Security, somebody we could fool completely. And we were wrong. She's good." He grinned. "But not quite good enough to get us all."

"Lucky for you," Morgenstein grumbled, but he was essentially correct. Shimoda had seemed to be the perfect idiot to run things into the ground, and she had surprised them all. "Well, we'll say no more about it. Meanwhile, I think it's time to get on with the last stage of the game. I put a call through to Mars, and the Administrator should be joining us quite shortly at this conference. I hope you all remember that due to the time delay for messages from Mars, he won't be able to talk directly to us, and you can't expect an immediate answer to any questions you pose him."

Right on cue, the holo-image of the Administrator formed in the room's only empty chair. He looked rather pleased with himself. "Good day, comrades," he said, nodding slightly at them all. "I am pleased to inform you that Mars is now under our control, and awaiting your arrival. You probably heard rumors and reports of a rebellion, but that has been completely crushed. All of the ringleaders are now in jail, awaiting execution. I want them to see Earth degenerate into chaos before I have them put to death." He paused, then added, "I am very sorry to report that two of the rebels are Charle Wilson and his adopted son, Jame."

Morgenstein started in shock at the news. Wilson had been something of an idealist, and had been recruited believing that Quietus was working for the betterment of the human race. He was expendable. But Jame . . .

"Jame is essential to our plans," Fried snapped, for once not playing with that stupid stylus of hers. "How did he become a rebel? And how can you even *think* of executing him?"

Quan agreed. "With Devon gone, we need one of our specially bred computer geniuses. Jame Wilson *must* be kept alive to work for us. We need a counteragent to the Doomsday Virus so that we can free the Net when it is time for our return to power on Earth. Wilson *must* design it for us."

Morgenstein scowled again. The Administrator had been specially selected for his post because he was a ruthless and ambitious man. But now she wondered if he was *too* ruthless, allowing his emotions to get in the way of his job. "We may be able to use his father as leverage, to keep Wilson in line," she said. "I want both of them to be kept alive until we reach Mars. And the rest of the family. If I recall correctly, Wilson has a baby sister. I'm sure he'll be most cooperative, to avoid anything happening to her."

It was a few minutes before the Administrator heard their comments and replied to them. He shook his head. "You don't understand," he informed them. "Jame Wilson took over the power systems of the cities. He's extremely dangerous to us. He *must* be executed, because we cannot trust him. I'm sure there must be other competent computer programmers we can use. What about the boy who foiled the first release of the Doomsday Virus? Can't we capture him and apply pressure on him to help us?"

"Idiot," Van Dreelen snapped. "He's on Earth, and is likely to die when the virus wipes out EarthNet. We need somebody on Mars, and that has to be Jame Wilson. I don't care how dangerous you think he is, we can bring him into line by pressuring his family. Now stop arguing, and get with it."

That was probably the best way to deal with a man like the Administrator, Morgenstein realized: give him no choice, and show him who is in charge. Maybe, when they reached Mars, he could meet with a slight but fatal accident? "It seems that everything is falling into place very well," she said. "I think that a toast is called for, my friends." She tapped a button on her desk-comp, and a waiter came in with a tray of champagne. He quietly and efficiently placed a glass beside every member of the committee, save the Administrator, and then left again.

Morgenstein stood up and raised her own glass. "Lady and gentlemen," she said, "I give you a toast to the future. Long may Quietus reign!" She smiled at the chorus of approval and sipped her champagne.

Then she noticed that Van Dreelen had made no

move to join the toast. "What is wrong?" she asked him. "Are you trying to annoy me, or do you have some objection to joining us for a toast?"

"Neither, really," Van Dreelen replied. He stood up and sighed. "Well, you were bound to discover the truth some time, so now is as good a time as any, I suppose." He moved his hand to the glass — and passed straight through it. He smiled slightly. "I'm not really with you, I'm afraid. You'll be making this journey without me."

Morgenstein stared at Van Dreelen in shock. He was a holo-image! But . . . how? And, more important, *why*? "Why aren't you with us?" she asked. "You were there on Overlook. I shook your hand!"

"I was on Overlook, true," Van Dreelen agreed. "I had to be physically present so you'd be sure about me. I needed you to tip your hands and assemble together on schedule." He smiled cheerfully. "I'm afraid I'm one of the good guys, after all."

Morgenstein whitened. "What are you talking about? You're one of the most important members of Quietus! You can't —"

"I *can*," he replied. "I'm the traitor you've all been looking for. And now, I'm afraid, I have some pressing business to attend to. Which, I promise you, you *won't* like." He moved to switch off his image, and then paused. "Oh, I wouldn't look too hard for the Doomsday Virus to destroy EarthNet, if I were you. It's not going to happen." His image vanished.

Morgenstein and the others stared at one another in silence. What was happening? And how would this affect their plans?

3

Shimoda stared at the figure of Van Dreelen, standing lazily in the doorway. "How dare you?" she
breathed. Her hand moved toward her desk-comp, to
send for shields to have the man arrested. What infer-
nal cheek he had, coming back like this! If he *had*
come back . . . "Are you a holo-image?"

Van Dreelen moved to join her. Then he gripped her
hand and bent to kiss it. "I'm here in the flesh," he
said. "But I'd hold off on having me arrested for a
while, my dear. You're really going to need what I've
brought for you."

"What are you talking about, you traitor?" Borden

growled. "You have the gall to betray us and then stroll in here, bold as brass, as if you're some kind of hero?"

"I *am* some kind of hero," Van Dreelen replied modestly. "You see, I'm not a traitor to Computer Control, but to Quietus."

"How can you expect us to believe such lies?" Copin demanded.

"Because I'm *here*," he pointed out. "Not on my way to Mars with those traitors. My plan has finally worked."

"Your plan?" asked Shimoda. Then she blinked, and pulled her hand from his grip, blushing slightly. "But he's right," she added to the rest of the room. "He *is* here, and not fleeing with the rest of the scum. Perhaps we should hear him out."

"That's my girl," Van Dreelen said, taking a seat beside her.

"I'm not your girl!" Shimoda shot back.

"I know." He sighed theatrically. "But I'm working on it. Anyway, where was I? Oh, yes, explaining why I shouldn't be sent to jail for the rest of my life, and why I should be listened to. Let me tell you a story. . . ."

He settled back comfortably in the chair. Shimoda stared at him, her emotions in turmoil. Could they believe him? Could *she* believe him? She'd been so certain for so long that he was in deep with Quietus. Was it at all possible that she'd been mistaken?

"I was approached to join Quietus fifteen years ago," he explained. "Ben Quan recruited me, when I was still head of Security myself. I decided that I had to listen to him, and found him outlining the most unbelievable plot against the human race. Even he, though, didn't know who all of his fellow conspirators were. My first instinct was to have him thrown into jail. Then I realized that this would accomplish nothing useful. I needed to know who else was in the conspiracy, and what they were doing. So I pretended to sympathize with their aims, and joined up.

"The problem is that they were such a paranoid bunch — with good reason, of course. If anyone knew who they were, they were in danger of being betrayed and going to Ice for the rest of their lives. So I couldn't discover who else was in the plot. But I was shown elements of what was being planned. The more I found out, the more worried I became.

"Quietus was planning for the long term. They aimed to control EarthNet, and thus control the world. To do that, they had an illegal cloning laboratory set up. The scientists there cross-spliced various strands of DNA to create the ultimate hacker, someone with computing literally in his genes. They were going to use a man known only to me as the Malefactor to raise the resulting child. The boy named Devon does exist."

"So we discovered," Shimoda said dryly. "Connor was telling the truth all along."

"Indeed he was," agreed Van Dreelen. "I knew that, of course. I realized that with Devon out there creating his Doomsday Virus one day, we'd need a counter to him. I didn't know where Devon was, or who the Malefactor was, so I couldn't find either. So what I did was to pose as a doctor, and I stole a second embryo from the facility. A third was taken and sent to Mars as a backup for Devon. We'll have to deal with that boy when the time comes. Anyway, I took the infant I'd stolen and, posing as a doctor, gave him into the custody of a young couple."

"Connor's parents?" Shimoda asked.

"Right. All you have to do is to contact them, and they will identify me as a Dr. Taru, who gave them their child. I'd researched the couple, and they'd just lost a real son. They were good and honest, a perfect pair to raise the boy, whom they named Tristan. Over the years, I checked up on him and saw that he'd become, as was genetically inevitable, quite a ferocious little programmer. I was sure that when the time came, I'd be able to contact him and set him onto Devon. As it happened, he found Devon before I had to get in touch with him, and started things off on his own."

"But how can we believe all of this?" Horesh, from

Development, demanded. "Do you have any proof for what you're claiming?"

"How could I have proof?" he asked her. "If I did, Quietus would have found it. All I can offer is that I'm *here*, with you, not on my way to Mars with them. Let me finish, and then you can decide whether to believe me or not. I had a lot to do in my attempt to expose and destroy Quietus. Peter Chen was considered as a member, but they realized he was too honest to be a part of the conspiracy. So it was decided to dispose of him. I actually framed him as a member of Quietus to get him out of here and keep him alive. And it gave me the chance to bring in my own choice for a replacement. Miss Shimoda."

"Why pick on me?" she asked.

"Two reasons, really. First, I could see that you were dedicated and relentless, even if the rest of Computer Control thought you'd messed up the hunt for the Doomsday Virus. You'd gotten so much closer than I had expected anyone could, and that impressed me. I knew you'd do a far better job than anyone would give you credit for."

"And the other reason?" asked Schein, from Customer Relations.

Van Dreelen grinned. "I happen to think she's a very attractive young lady, and I'm still hoping that when

25

everything's finished, she'll agree to go to dinner with me. I'm an unbridled optimist, you see."

Shimoda blushed again. He certainly had nerve, whichever side he was on! "You may yet be in jail when all of this is over," she pointed out.

"Oh, I don't think so," he said airily. "But if I am, we can have dinner together in my cell, surely?"

"I have more important things to think about right now," she said, trying to sound cold.

"Fair enough," he agreed, smiling lazily. "Anyway, your idea of giving everybody Truzac to find out who they were loyal to really scared me. You thought it was because it would prove that I was a member of Quietus, of course. But it was the exact opposite. You'd have exposed me as a traitor to Quietus, and that would have ended my effectiveness. Probably my life, too. So I couldn't allow you to do it." He shrugged. "I'd be happy to take the stuff now, though, to convince you that I'm telling the truth."

"I'll consider it," Shimoda promised, and meant it. Maybe that would be the only way to be sure about him.

"I had to let them play out their hand," Van Dreelen continued. "It was the only way I'd be able to discover who they really were, and to isolate them where they couldn't do anyone any harm — on a spaceship bound for Mars. Now they're there, helpless. All we have to do is arrest the lot of them."

"There's just one small problem with that," growled Rodriguez, head of Programming. "We can't find them. They're hidden from radar."

Van Dreelen grinned. "Yes, that was rather clever of them, wasn't it? And setting up a fake ship for Miss Shimoda to attack and capture? Don't forget, they are all very clever." His grin widened. "Fortunately, not as clever as me. You see, I went to Overlook in person to greet them and pretended to get on their ship with them. Instead, I immediately returned to Earth to join you here. Oh, yes, that reminds me — I borrowed a shield Ramjet for this. You'll find the records at the airport to confirm that part of my story. Anyway, I used a holo-projector to send an image of myself to join them on the ship. Sadly, they discovered the truth, so now they know I'm with you again, and not one of them."

"How could you do that?" asked Copin, frowning. "If their ship is shielded against detection, you couldn't have sent a signal to them for the holo-image to ride." Van Dreelen continued to grin at her. "Unless," she suddenly realized, "you had some sort of transmitter aboard the ship to home in on."

Van Dreelen applauded slowly. "I did indeed. And it's

still there and operating. All you need to know is the frequency, and you can track that ship down and capture the whole lot of them."

Shimoda stared at him in surprise and hope. "You really did that?"

"I really did. Are you proud of me?" he asked modestly.

"If you're telling the truth, it's wonderful," she said.

Van Dreelen grinned. "Well, at least we won't have to put up with all that petty bickering while we work now." He rubbed his hands together. "Right, let's do what we can. Get onto Peter Chen and that Lieutenant Barnes of yours on Overlook."

Shimoda tapped through the call, and the Screen leaped to immediate life. "Jill, Peter," she said. "We've had a small breakthrough." She brought them up to date on the Devon situation, and then Van Dreelen moved to join her.

"Now, something to keep you busy," he told them. He sent them a signal. "That has the frequency of the transponder I planted on Quan," he explained. "Tap into it, and you can capture the members of Quietus."

"Terrific," Chen said.

"We're ready to move," Barnes added. "They won't get away, I promise."

"Excellent." Shimoda managed a wan smile. "Let us

28

know when you have them. Do whatever you have to."
She cut the signal, and looked at Van Dreelen. "That
solves one of our problems."

"One of them?" Van Dreelen's smile vanished. "What
are you talking about?"

"You missed the discussion that was going on just
before you arrived," Shimoda informed him. "Devon's
resurfaced, and wants to be handed total power of
Earth. Or else he's going to destroy every living thing on
the planet." Seeing his shocked expression, she brought
him up to date.

"The filthy little rat," Van Dreelen said, clenching
his fists. "Taki, I had no idea he'd turn out to be this
dangerous. Or this insane. If I had, I'd have worked
harder at tracking him down. I thought that Quietus was
the real menace, and I concentrated on them. I'm
sorry."

He'd called her by her first name . . . Shimoda pushed
her emotions to one side for now. "I believe you," she
said. It all made a convoluted kind of sense, and he
was here, after all, when he didn't need to be. "And
you've done wonders. But Devon is the most important
problem we have right now."

"You're dead right I am."

Shimoda and the others whirled around, to see the
holo-projection of Devon, seated and munching peanut

29

nukes. "So," he continued, stuffing his mouth, "have you made up your minds yet? Do I get to be emperor of Earth, or do you all get to be deep-fried?"

Shimoda's mouth went dry. Borden leaned forward. "We were about to take a vote on the matter," he said carefully, reining in his emotions. "Perhaps we could do that right this moment?" He looked around the room. "All of those in favor of giving the Omega Circuit to Devon, raise your hands."

Jada's hand inched upward very hesitantly. Shimoda kept both of her clenched fists firmly on the table. Van Dreelen smiled wanly, placed one of his hands over hers, and kept the other one down.

Nobody else raised a hand. Jada looked around the room, sweat trickling. "Don't be stupid! We have to do it, or Earth dies!"

"I'd sooner it die," Horesh said coldly, "than let that pond scum there have control over us all."

"So would we all, I believe," Borden added, his face tense.

"What's wrong with you?" Devon yelled, spilling the bowl of peanuts. It vanished from his image as it fell to the ground. "Don't you think I'll do it?"

"I'm sure you will," Shimoda replied, a tight knot of fear and determination in her stomach. "But that's better than letting you control Earth. You're insane, and you'd simply abuse your power. You'd torture people and kill them for your own amusement."

"Of course I would," Devon said, surprised. "Why else would I be playing this game?"

"It's not a game," Van Dreelen snapped. "This is deadly serious, Devon. You have to stop it. Now."

"Nobody tells me what to do," Devon said. "You won't let me rule Earth? Fine. Your decision. But that simply means that I win the game anyway. The garbage ship is going to crash into Earth's atmosphere and kill the lot of you. And good riddance to you all! Wimps!" His image vanished.

Shimoda was sweating, too, now. She looked around the room, a terrible pain in her heart. "We may just have signed Earth's death warrant," she said softly.

"Better that than become his playthings," Borden assured her. He glared at Jada. "Coward. Perhaps you'd better leave. And if you say a word about this to anyone, I promise you that you'll die a little ahead of the rest of us." Wordlessly, Jada got up and stalked out of the room.

Van Dreelen sighed and closed his eyes. "I thought I'd be returning a hero. Instead, I'm just another victim." He looked at Shimoda. "How long do we have?"

"Less than six hours," she replied.

He nodded. "Time for a very nice meal, if we hurry. I

31

still want to get in at least one dinner with you before we die."

Shimoda threw her hands up. "Can't you take this seriously?"

"Believe me, I'm very serious. I think better on a full stomach. And if I'm going to die, I can't imagine a better way to go than in the company of a beautiful lady."

"Think better?" Shimoda focused on that. "You think there's a way out?"

"I don't know," Van Dreelen admitted. "But I'm not giving up hope while I'm still alive. I really think that the two of us might be able to think of something." He shrugged. "And the very least we can do with the time is to arrest Quietus. Whether we live or die, they can't be allowed to go free."

Shimoda nodded. Though she didn't feel at all brilliant right now, she knew that he was right. They couldn't give up until the very end. "Very well," she agreed. "I, too, think better when my stomach isn't growling for food."

"There you go," Van Dreelen said approvingly. "I knew I didn't really have to be the last man alive on Earth for you to go out with me. Though I'm getting uncomfortably close . . ."

4

evon was furious. He threw the bowl of peanut nukes across the room. It was duraplastic, so it didn't break. Viciously, he kicked at his chair, and almost succeeded in breaking his foot. Hobbling, he sat down again, ignoring the pain in his toes because of the rage in his heart.

It was that stupid shield woman's fault! *She* had convinced the rest of them to stand up to him! He'd looked in on plenty of Computer Control meetings in the past, and he'd never seen them behaving like this. Normally they just complained and grumbled and politely insulted

33

one another. Now, with this Shimoda woman aboard, they had actually taken a stand! When he'd first seen the shield, Devon had thought she was dull and incompetent, but perhaps amusing.

She'd stopped being amusing now.

Should he kill her? It wouldn't be too difficult, after all. Just a small "malfunction" in the equipment she used somewhere along the line. Electrify a floor square in her office, for example. Or send a noxious gas into her air supply. Or just lock the door and leave her to rot . . . Each image was quite pleasing. But then Devon realized it was really rather futile. She was going to die with everyone else anyway, and killing her now would only spare her the fear of impending doom. Why spare her that pain?

They weren't playing fair! He'd won, and they were supposed to realize it and back down. How *dare* they suddenly find the backbone to stand up to him? He stared out of the viewer at Earth, looming large ahead of him now. Just a few more hours, and it would all be dead. Oh, he'd go through with his threat if he had to. If he didn't, nobody would ever believe his word again. But really, he didn't *want* to kill the human race just yet. He wanted to keep them as his playthings, and they weren't going to be much fun if they were dead. He wanted them alive, with him in complete control. But those miserable idiots on the board wouldn't let him have what he wanted.

He knew *exactly* what he had to do: go over their heads. They were keeping a news clamp on this story, so they were the only ones on Earth who knew about its impending destruction. Smart, from their point of view, to avoid panic. On the other hand, from *his* point of view, it was an opportunity. . . . The Computer Control people ultimately had to answer to the public for what they did. All the public needed to know was the truth.

Besides, once the general population knew that they were doomed, there would be a lot of wonderful panic. He was bound to get some great news footage of stupidity, death, and disaster. He'd make the Stock Market Panic of '17 look like a pleasant afternoon picnic. . . .

With luck, there would be enough public outcry that the board would be compelled to give in to his demands and make him emperor of Earth after all. If not, at least he'd get some amusement out of humanity's last hours.

Happy again, he set about downloading all of his conversations with Computer Control and sent them to all the NetNews stations. . . .

This was the second time Tristan had been into space, but it wasn't as exciting as the first. The transport ship he, Genia, and Mora were on wasn't equipped for the comfort of passengers, so there was nothing to see or do, really. Captain O'Connell was gruff but nice enough, and the other crew member, Brightman, talked only when addressed. That meant that Tristan was left alone with Mora and Genia for the most part. Once upon a time, he'd have thought being alone with two very attractive young women would be the next best thing to being in heaven.

Now he knew better.

Mora was touching up her makeup. She'd always prided herself on the neatness of her appearance. Her eyebrows were neatly trimmed, her makeup slight but effective, her lips glossed and shining. She must have really loathed being in the Underworld, where she not only couldn't find food or shelter, but must have been filthy and unwashed.

Genia, on the other hand, ignored makeup entirely. She had let her hair grow out into a long, bushy mane that was really very fetching. It would be impractical if she lived Above, of course — too many stray hairs and chances that a thief might get a sample of her DNA from it. But since she had no Implant Chip, she wasn't bothered about such things. Her only condescension to fashion was that she liked to wear rather garish clothing. Right now, she had on a shimmering silver top and long, shiny black pants that clung to her figure very well.

If only she wasn't so hung up on Tristan being two years younger than her . . . and if only she and Mora could get along better.

"It's no good," Genia said to the other girl. "Nothing you do improves the picture much."

Mora glared at her. "*You* could do with a makeover yourself. Running hard into a brick wall might improve you. But I don't think *anything* could improve your taste in clothing."

"I haven't heard Tristan complaining about what I wear," Genia snapped. "In fact, he seems to find the view rather pleasant, considering how often he's looking at me." Tristan flushed; he hadn't been aware he was that obvious.

"Well, that's probably because you're leaving very little to his imagination!" Mora exclaimed. "Don't you have any modesty?"

Genia laughed, and gestured at Mora's one-piece, slightly baggy umber jumpsuit. "I think you've got enough for the two of us, Miss Prissy. I'll stick with what I like, thanks."

Tristan had learned by now not to get into the middle

of their fights. If he did, they both verbally savaged him. So, trying to drown them out, he connected with Earth-Net and surfed for news.

He almost fell out of his seat with shock.

"Shut up, both of you!" he ordered. To his surprise, they did just that, and turned to look at him. "Come and see this." He turned his Screen so they could both watch, and then refreshed the news. For once, the two girls stayed absolutely silent as they watched the broadcast of Devon's showdown with Computer Control. At the end of it, the three of them simply looked at one another in dead silence.

"Can he do it?" asked Genia eventually. Her voice was cracking.

"He wouldn't have threatened it otherwise," Tristan said soberly. "He's arrogant and egotistical, but he's not a liar. He doesn't need to be."

"Do you think Computer Control can stop him?" Mora wanted to know.

"No." Tristan was too depressed to try to sugarcoat the truth. "They'll try, I'm sure of that. But they'll never be able to outsmart him."

Mora glared at him. "Only you can save the world, is that it?" she snapped.

"I've got the best chance," Tristan replied honestly.

"I've been engineered to be as smart as him. If he can do this, I should be able to undo it."

"Plus, you've got me to help, and he doesn't," Genia added. She glanced at Mora. "Of course, we've got her to hinder us, and Devon doesn't, so I suppose that might even out."

"This isn't time for your usual fighting," Tristan said firmly. "Okay, we're going to have to start working on this one, and we're going to need Captain O'Connell's help if we can come up with something. Genia, can you go up to the flight deck and bring her up to date? See if she'd be willing to bend the rules and give us a hand if we need it."

"Why me?" asked Genia. "Why not Miss Useless there?"

"Because you've got a better chance of explaining it to her and convincing her," Tristan said. "After all, you're a con and a thief by profession; talking her into helping us out should be a snap."

Genia nodded. "Good thinking." She shot for the door and left.

Mora pouted. "You really are hot for her, aren't you? I notice you didn't trust *me* with that job."

"It was because I wanted her out of the way," Tristan explained. "I knew she'd object to what I'm about to do now." He turned back to his comp and typed in his access codes that he'd stolen from Shimoda, so he could hack into the shield computers. Then he sent out a call for her.

"Do you think it's smart, contacting the shields?" Mora asked.

"Considering I'm on their most-wanted list, no," Tristan admitted. "But I don't have any choice. Ah." The call went through, and the Screen lit up. Shimoda was staring at him, amazed. He couldn't be certain, but it looked like she was in a restaurant, eating dinner.

"Connor!" she exclaimed. "I didn't expect to hear from you!"

"I didn't expect to call," he confessed. "But I have no choice. You've seen what Devon is broadcasting?"

"Yes," she answered grimly. "And, as I'm sure he wanted, there's panic under way down here. It's getting very ugly. I suspect he hoped to pressure us into giving in to his demands."

Tristan shook his head. "Don't," he urged her. "He'll only make everyone wish they were dead."

"We kind of figured that out." Shimoda's face softened slightly. "Why did you call?"

Tristan hesitated and swallowed. This was the hard part, the bit he knew Genia would probably beat him over the head with a sharp object for. "I'm willing to give myself up," he told her. "But you have to trust me first, and let me help stop Devon."

A man's voice broke into the conversation. "No deal." Shimoda moved over to show she was with a handsome-looking man a bit older than she was. Tristan was stunned; he'd expected them to be willing to negotiate. Now what was he going to do? The man half smiled. "Tristan, for a genius, you don't think things through very well. Devon's confessed that he created the Doomsday Virus. You're free; you've been officially exonerated and pardoned. We don't want to arrest you anymore."

"You don't?" Tristan had been running for so long, he could hardly believe it.

"We'd be more than happy to accept your help," Shimoda confirmed. "And we'll do what we can to help you out." She glanced around. "Um, this restaurant is a trifle public for this. Can you hold on a moment?" The picture froze for about thirty seconds, and then re-formed at a fresh location. Tristan realized it was now coming from inside the ladies' room at the restaurant.

The man grinned. "I always wondered what the inside of one of these places looked like."

"Keep your mind on the job," Shimoda warned him, and turned back to Tristan. "What do you need?"

"Do you have any idea where that Doomsday ship

41

is?" he asked. "Or the one that Devon is in? All I gathered was that both are heading toward Earth, but space is pretty huge."

"No idea at all, I'm afraid," Shimoda replied. "If we had, we'd shoot the things down. We've taken a couple of nuclear missiles out of storage for just that purpose. But we don't have a target for them."

Tristan winced; it had been a long shot, but he had been hoping it might pay off. "Then I guess we'll have to do this the hard way. How long, exactly, do we have?"

"As of now? Five and a half hours." Shimoda grimaced. "But we really wouldn't like to cut it too close."

"I know what you mean," Tristan said. "I don't know if we'll be able to stop him. But we'll try."

"Good luck." Shimoda paused. "And, Tristan — I'm sorry for not believing you earlier. And for what I've put you through."

Tristan half smiled. "Don't worry about it. Maybe I'll InstaSue you — if I save the world." He switched off and sighed, looking at Mora. "Well, it looks like we'd better get busy."

"We?" asked Mora, slightly huffily. "That girlfriend of yours thinks I'm about as much use as a 1999 iMac."

"She's not my girlfriend," Tristan protested. "And I don't agree with her about everything. I'm sure you'll be able to help out."

"If she's not your girlfriend," Mora grumbled, "she sure acts like she owns you."

"That's because she's a thief, and she's used to taking things that aren't tied down. Anyway, let's see if she's convinced the captain to help."

They headed for the bridge, where grim faces showed him that Genia had at least clued in O'Connell and Brightman. She looked around as Tristan and Mora entered. "What's the news?"

"Not good." Tristan filled the three of them in. "Devon's masked his radar signals," he concluded. "We can't detect either ship. Unless we can figure out how to intercept them without being able to detect them, we don't have a chance."

The captain shook her head. "That's the problem with you nonspacers," she remarked. "You always make space sound like it's some kind of a problem. You really don't understand it, do you?"

"No," Tristan admitted.

"And I'll bet this clone sibling of yours is just as ignorant." O'Connell sighed and started tapping on her nav-comp. "Look, to get from the Moon to Earth, there are only so many ways of doing it, given the data we have. We know when the ship launched from the Moon, and when it quit lunar orbit. That gives us a starting point. We know when it's due to reach Earth, and what its maximum thrust is. With all of this, working out where it must be is a breeze, trust me. We don't need to get it on radar." Her fingers worked feverishly, and she ended up with a short sectional cone stretching out from Earth.

"That's still a big area to search," Mora objected, looking at it.

"We refine it," the captain stated. She tapped more keys, and a small sphere blinked into existence, just inside the narrow part of the cone. "Overlook," she explained. "Devon won't want to get his ship too close to that, in case it's picked up visually. So we scrub its area of sight, and we're left with . . ." The cone narrowed considerably. "Right, given the timing of the ship, it should be about . . . here." A small red image started blinking. "A search area for us of only about a hundred cubic miles. With luck, we could spot its thrusters. Without luck, we have to search a bit."

"Can't we bounce a signal around in that space?" asked Genia. "Catch it by reflection?"

"It's treated against radar," Mora pointed out.

Genia sighed. "Radar's not the only thing we can use. The ship's filled with radioactive ores. If we can use a small electron particle beam, it should be absorbed by the ship, or partially reflected. We could use one to scan for the craft."

44

O'Connell looked interested. "It might work at that, kid. Maybe you and Brightman could cobble something together? I'm going to be busy putting us on what I hope will be an intercept course with this flying bomb." She glanced at Tristan as she started reworking their position and course. "You think you can stop it once we get there?"

"I don't know," he admitted honestly. "But I'm hoping that if Devon can program it, I can deprogram it."

"Well, we'll all hope along with you, then," O'Connell answered. "But . . ." She grimaced. "If we find that ship, I can't let it continue on course. If you can't defuse it, or alter its trajectory, then we have to destroy it before it reaches Earth. And I don't think we'll have enough time to get away. You catch my meaning?"

Tristan nodded slowly as he contemplated the point. If he couldn't stop the ship, O'Connell would use the *Simón Bolívar* as a bomb itself, to blow up the death ship.

And kill all of them with it.

5

Jame was slumped in his cell, horribly depressed and defeated. The rebellion against the corrupt Administrator was over, and they had lost. The Administrator's threat to destroy the power stations — which would kill everyone on Mars in a short while — had been sincere and effective. Captain Montrose had been forced to surrender to the Earth shields. The rebels, including Jame's mother and his baby sister, Fai, had all been locked away in separate cells. The Administrator had made it clear that he intended to execute them all just as soon as Quietus had destroyed EarthNet and set their own plans for dominating mankind too far into motion for them ever to be stopped.

He wasn't depressed for himself as much as for his sister. She was just a baby, and had so much to look forward to, if only she lived. But the Administrator had made it clear that she would be shot, too, along with the rest of the rebels, as an example to everyone on Mars. Nobody would ever dare rebel again. Jame was sure the Administrator was probably right in his estimate. Technically, of course, Fai wasn't exactly his sister, since he had been adopted as a baby. Jame had discovered that he was a clone, one of three that existed. He wondered what his "brothers" were like. He'd never have the chance to meet them and find out. In a short while, he'd be dead.

It was hard to imagine being dead. He'd almost been executed once already, but had been saved by Montrose. That had scared him, but now he was almost shaking. There was so much to look forward to, so much that he would never know. He felt sorry for these lost opportunities, but he refused to panic or beg for his life. Some things weren't worth the price. He would do his best to accept fate, and die with dignity.

If he could just stop shaking.

The door to his small cell opened, and an armed shield came in. The man's face was blank as he ordered Jame to accompany him.

Was this it? Was he to be executed now? Trying not to shake, Jame stood up, dragging together every last ounce of his courage. Slowly, he walked beside the shield, turning when the man ordered him to. He tried to blank out his mind, to not panic. It wasn't easy, but at least it kept his mind focused on the present, and not on what was to come.

Suddenly, as they walked through a doorway, Jame realized where he was: in the Administrator's offices. He blinked, confused. The guard prodded him to keep walking. Surely the Administrator wasn't going to have Jame executed in his own office, was he? Aside from anything else, it would make a mess on the floor.

What was happening? For a moment, Jame felt a surge of hope. Had the tyrant changed his mind? Or was this part of some devious plan?

The door opened, and the guard pushed Jame through, into the Administrator's private office. It was large and opulent, the man having spared no expense on his own comforts. There was a large desk and comp station at one end, and then couches, tables, statues, and buffets ranged about the rest of the room. The Administra-

48

tor was at his desk, and looked up with a scowl as Jame was pushed in to meet him.

"This wasn't my idea," he complained. "But there's a job for you to do."

Jame almost laughed in the man's face. "You expect me to work for you?" he asked. He shook his head. "No way."

"This isn't for me," the Administrator answered, getting to his feet. "It's for Earth."

"What are you talking about?" Jame was very confused now. This had to be some sort of a trick.

"Just shut up and watch this," the Administrator ordered. He called up a picture on the large Screen beside his desk, and gestured for Jame to pay attention.

It was the most incredible film Jame had ever seen. A boy — who looked exactly like Jame — threatened to destroy Earth. Computer Control refused to negotiate with him. The film ended, and the Administrator scowled.

Jame stared at him. "That boy," he said finally. "He's one of my clone brothers, isn't he?"

"Yes." The Administrator started pacing the floor. "He's the computer genius Quietus was raising to develop the Doomsday Virus we would use to take over Earth. But he's become . . . unstable. Unusable. Quietus wants Earth intact and subdued. We cannot allow Devon to destroy humanity."

"Right," Jame said dryly. "No slaves if they're all gone, eh?"

"He's insane," the Administrator stated.

"I think that's the first thing you've said that I completely agree with." Jame studied the man, and realized he was scared. An interesting turn of events. Jame was even more scared. Now he had the future of the whole human race to consider, not just those on Mars. "But why am I here?"

"You were raised to be a computer genius, too," the Administrator informed him. "The plan was that you would be activated should anything happen to Devon. Something *has* happened to him, and he's gone too far. You're the only person who can possibly think enough like him to stop him now. It's no longer for Quietus, but for the human race. You can't refuse to do it."

Jame shook his head, incredulous. "You want *me* to figure out how to stop Devon from destroying Earth?" He laughed, more from nerves than amusement. "Quite a hope! What can I do from here?"

"I don't know," the Administrator admitted. "To be frank, I was against letting you even try. I don't trust you at all."

"And you no longer have any hold over me, do you?"

asked Jame. "After all, you've condemned my family to death already. And my friends. I've nothing else left to lose but my own life, and you aim to cut that short, too." He raised an eyebrow. "So why are you doing this?"

"I've been ordered to do so," the Administrator said with distaste. "And to offer you and your family a reprieve if you succeed."

"Too kind of you," Jame mocked. "Frankly, I don't think I can trust you at all. I don't believe you'll spare us."

Oddly, the Administrator looked slightly relieved. "So you're refusing to even try?"

"I didn't say that." Jame stared at the Screen. "Unlike you, I have ethics. I can't allow Earth to die if I can do anything to save it. Give me computer access, and I promise I'll do my best to stop Devon. Understand, I'm not promising results — just my best shot."

The Administrator scowled again. "I have no option but to allow you to try," he said. "But I'm going to have you watched at all times. If you try anything . . ."

"What?" Jame was amused. "You'll have me shot? You're planning on doing that anyway. You can't threaten me any longer."

The Administrator gave a nasty smile. "Oh, I think I can. You're rather attached to that little sister of yours, aren't you?"

Jame's blood chilled. "You've already condemned her to death," he said, feeling sick.

"Well, I can postpone that fate awhile," the man answered, knowing he'd found Jame's weakness. "If we find you doing anything at all wrong, she'll be tortured."

"You're *sick*," Jame spat, horrified.

"I'm effective," the Administrator answered, certain he'd cornered Jame at last. "Do what you can to save Earth — and *nothing* else. Or your baby sister will face a lot of pain." He turned away, smug in his own schemes.

Jame closed his eyes and leaned over the computer console. *Forgive me, Fai*, he prayed silently. Hurting her was almost the last thing he would ever want to do.

But there was one thing he couldn't allow: He could *never* leave a monster like the Administrator in charge here. Even if he was discovered and Fai suffered, Jame had to stop him somehow. . . .

He bent to his task, trying to clear all his worries and fears from his mind. The first thing he had to do was find Devon. His sibling-clone had masked his ship, but there were other ways to detect him. The most obvious to Jame's mind was through the vids he'd sent to the NewsNets. He would have had to access them from whatever ship he was using. No doubt Devon had hidden his trail, but if he truly was Jame's double, then

Jame had a good idea how he might have gone about it. With luck, he could then backtrack the signals.

It meant using his snakes to go out into the Net and search for the identifying patterns. He didn't dare tap into EarthNet; the Doomsday Virus was loose there, and he didn't want to get caught in that. But one of the sites used was Overlook's public station, and he worked from that. As he did so, he keyed in a command for one of his snakes to go off on a separate mission. The Administrator had claimed that he'd mined the power plants of the Martian cities, and would explode them if Earth interfered with him. Jame needed to know if that was true before he could make any further plans. He hid this search among the others, knowing that it would take a lot of scanning and checking of what he was doing to find it.

Tracking down Devon wasn't going to be simple, though. Jame concentrated on the job, piecing things together bit by bit. One little piece of data here, one small line of encryption there . . . If Devon had created it, Jame was almost certain he could backtrack it.

Almost.

As he worked, his snake reported back: The Administrator *had* been telling the truth. All of the power plants now had bombs attached to them — relatively crude ones that could be triggered by a simple radio command. Jame glanced at the man who was pacing the room, casting the occasional look in Jame's direction. He'd have the trigger on him, somewhere. Most likely in his wrist-comp. No way of preventing him from getting to it, Jame realized. And he was absolutely certain that if anything went wrong, the maniac would send the signal, condemning everyone on Mars to death.

Since he couldn't stop the signal from being sent, Jame knew his only chance was to make certain that it wouldn't be effective. Because the Administrator was an arrogant but not terribly bright man, that was something very simple to do. While he was changing the frequency codes in his hunt for Devon, Jame slipped in commands to do the same thing for the bombs. He almost held his breath while he waited to see what would happen, except that he knew this might alert the Administrator that there was something wrong. Instead, he kept working away, keeping an eye on what was happening with the bombs.

Thirty seconds later, his snake was finished. The bomb arming codes had been changed, and now only Jame had them. The Administrator could send as many signals as he liked — it wouldn't do him any good, because Jame had locked down the explosives. They would still look like they were armed, but he'd be the only one who could set them off. That was one major headache out of the way, and Jame sighed with relief.

Which was a major mistake.

The Administrator looked at him sharply. "What have you done?" he demanded.

For a second, Jame was utterly sick; if the Administrator discovered that the bombs had been disarmed, all he had to do was to plant new ones, and everything Jame had done would be useless. It was so *stupid* of him to act so happy!

And then the Screen lit up with an all-too-familiar face. It was like looking at himself.

Devon.

The Administrator clearly thought *this* was why Jame had looked happy, and the suspicious expression was wiped from his face. Devon, however, looked totally startled.

"Tristan!" he exclaimed. "How did you get through to me?"

"I'm not Tristan," Jame replied. "I'm Jame Wilson."

"Oh, great." Devon rolled his eyes. "The other Devon wannabe. Sorry, I can't stay to chat. I'm rather busy."

"Trying to destroy Earth?" Jame asked. "No way, Devon."

Devon snorted. "And who are *you* to tell me what to do? I don't take orders from anybody."

The Administrator moved forward. "You take them from me," he said coldly. "From Quietus. I'm ordering you to stop this radioactive bomb of yours. We do not want Earth destroyed, merely immobilized."

Devon looked amused. "Hello! Didn't you hear me, zero gravity? I said I don't take orders from *anybody*. Not that I figure you're anybody in particular. As for Quietus, it can go rot for all I care. I'm through with that bunch of jerks. The future belongs to me, and me alone."

"I can't let you do that," Jame said firmly.

"You can't *stop* me," Devon pointed out. "Besides, a couple of hours from now, Earth will be dead anyway. Unless they wise up and make me their ruler."

Jame couldn't believe this boy who looked like him. "What you're doing is *wrong*," he snapped.

Devon laughed. "Oh, spare me the lectures! You're as much of a pain as that other clone. Get this straight, dumbo — I'm the smartest mind there is around, and I deserve to be in charge. And if I'm not given my due, I'll destroy everyone."

Jame glanced at the Administrator. "I think he's related to you, not me," he muttered. "The same paranoid obsessions and stupid ambitions." His fingers flew over the speedboard. Now that he was into Devon's computer systems, he had to simply take them over. If he could lock Devon out, then Jame could take control of the bomb ship, as well as Devon's ship.

The trouble was, Devon was as smart as Jame, and could see what was happening. He grinned and tapped a short command into his Terminal.

A huge dragon's head suddenly reared out of the Screen, and Jame leaped back in shock. The Administrator howled in terror. A second later, Jame's heart stopped racing, and he realized it had just been a holo-projection Devon had sent along the carrier wave. Devon was laughing.

"Think yourself lucky," he said. "That could have been the Doomsday Virus. I could have wiped out MarsNet and killed you all. You want to know why I didn't?"

"Do tell," Jame said, through clenched teeth. Devon had broken his snake probe, and Jame wanted to reestablish it.

"Because if I wipe out Earth, I'm going to need somewhere to run. And that leaves only you guys."

"Aren't you forgetting the Moon?" Jame asked.

"No," Devon said. "Keep your eyes on that place. There's going to be a nice, spectacular series of explosions from there in a few hours. The people there are *boring*, and don't deserve to live."

"You're going to kill everyone there, too?" Jame

couldn't believe how insane his clone must be to think like this.

"Trust me, the Universe won't miss those short circuits." Devon waved his hand. "Sorry, but I'm kind of busy. See you later — when I'm ready to take you over." He cut the line and scrambled the link.

Jame cursed and hammered his fists on the desk. It would take him forever to reconnect now that Devon knew he was being hunted. He'd blown it, his only chance to save Earth.

And now Devon was thinking of conquering Mars. The Administrator was bad enough. But Devon would be a hundred times worse. Jame had to do something to stop all of this.

But what?

6

Back on the Moon, Moss looked around the alcove at the three engineers he'd brought out to the reactor room. They were standing close to the controlling computer, and Devon's little addition was quite evident to them all. It hadn't been easy to see what it was up to, because none of them had dared to tap directly into it. Instead, the chief engineer had managed to rig up a remote probe on a stand some ten feet away.

"What do you think?" Moss asked, his voice soft. He knew he was overreacting, but somehow he couldn't bring himself to raise his voice this close to an explosive device.

"It looks bad, sir," the chief engineer replied. "The device has a lock on the system. If we try to remove it, it will trigger a massive fuel dump that will cause an explosion. If we try to interfere with it, the same thing. And if we leave it alone, it's increasing the fuel mixture slowly. The midnight deadline is very real."

"Fine," Moss said tightly. "Now that you've confirmed the worst, what are our options here? Do we *have* any options?"

"Evacuation," one of the other engineers suggested.

Moss sighed. "To where?" he asked. "We can't get into ships, because the docks were all damaged. And there's not exactly anywhere safe to walk out there!" He gestured toward the barren, airless lunar surface. "I think we need a more realistic option. What can we do to ensure that the reactors don't explode?"

The three engineers looked at one another, and Moss could see that they didn't have a lot to offer. "Any ideas?" he asked.

"Just one," the female engineer said. "The device is causing the problem and potential explosion because it's changing the mix flow. Now, we can't override the flow commands, because the device will compensate and flood the reactor. But what if we simply stop the flow? Cut it off at the source. If there's no flow at all, then the device can't make it explode."

Moss thought about it for a second, then nodded vigorously. "That sounds perfectly workable," he agreed. Then, seeing their worried expressions, he slowed his enthusiasm down. "I assume your faces mean there's a problem with that solution?"

"A big one," the chief engineer answered. "If we close down the flow, it will shut off the reactors. There will be no power whatsoever for any of the lunar cities. And you know what that will mean."

Moss did indeed: *Everything* on the Moon depended upon power. The air wouldn't circulate or get purified; water wouldn't flow; the cities would start to lose heat, which couldn't be replaced. Nothing would work at all. "So we can't do it?"

"I think we can," the chief replied. "It's a matter of timing. The critical deadline for these devices is midnight. Once that moment comes, the devices will stop working, their tasks complete. What we have to do is shut off the flow before midnight and then start it up again afterward. Then we can recommence power generation."

"So where's the hitch?" asked Moss.

"We can't leave the devices active too close to the midnight deadline," the woman explained. "By that time, the reactors will be overheated, and pumping the reactants into a hot reactor would probably cause them to explode anyway."

"What we need," the chief added, "is a cool-down period for the reactors. We have to turn off the flow and shut the reactors down by ten. Then we can restart them shortly after midnight."

"Two hours without power?" Moss stared at the engineers. "Do you think we can survive it?"

"No," the woman admitted. "Not as we are. We have to shut down as much as we can before ten, to lower power drain. We can divert the power to emergency batteries. Maybe enough to last two hours on air recirculation. We won't choke to death. But we can't keep the heaters going, because they simply take too much energy. We'll be able to breathe, but we may freeze."

"That sounds like at least a partial plan," Moss said. He considered the problem for a moment. "Okay, how about if we order everyone evacuated to the meeting chambers, and close down air flow to the rest of the cities? This way, we're dealing with a smaller area, less power drain."

"That would help," the second man agreed. "And the sooner, the better. We have to start switching off the power to the domiciles and to nonessential work areas.

If you can get people moving to a communal area, we'll target that for priority."

"Will it be enough?" Moss wanted to know.

"Nobody's ever tried to shut down a lunar city and restart it, sir," the chief answered. "This is the first time ever. We'll know if it works as we do it. There's no other way. We either live to midnight or die trying."

Moss wished that they had a better hope, but he could see that this was all they could do. Finally, he nodded. "I'll start the evacuation," he promised. "You begin the shutdown. We're going to have to chance this, because nothing else at all is going to work. And let's just pray it's effective. It's all we have left now."

Tristan jumped as the instruments started showing a reaction. Genia yelled with pleasure, and even Brightman managed to crack a smile.

"We've found it," Genia announced. "The signal's weak, but it's definitely real. It's the garbage scow."

O'Connell fed the figures into the nav-comp. "It's reachable," she decided. "We can rendezvous with it in less than an hour. It'll take a genius to manage to maneuver, so you're lucky I'm aboard." She started to program in the course change. "But then what?"

"We have to get aboard it," Tristan announced. He

looked up from the communications panel, where he'd been working. "Devon's cut off all communication ability for the ship, so that nobody can send any signals to it."

O'Connell scowled. "Then how would he defuse it if Earth accepts his terms for surrender?"

"Presumably his ship is close by, and can get him here to do it," Tristan answered. "Assuming, of course, that he has any real intention of stopping it. He's just sick enough to destroy Earth no matter what the human race decides. He likes to have power over people, and this annihilation is the ultimate power, isn't it?"

"Yes." The captain scratched her neck. "We have to get you onto the ship, so you can deprogram it, or whatever you're going to do."

"And me," Genia put in. "He's going to need my help."

"I guess I go, too," Mora added.

"No!" O'Connell said sharply. "Look, kids, I don't suppose any of you have ever had any spacewalking experience, have you?" She stared hard at them.

Tristan shook his head. He'd "walked" on plenty of other worlds in VR, but had absolutely no experience with the real thing. Genia and Mora both shook their heads, too.

"That's what I figured. Believe me, it's not the simplest thing to do." O'Connell glanced at her crew member. "Brightman, you're going to have to suit up and go with them, baby them along. You may need to get them into the ship."

Brightman nodded. "I could do with a bit of exercise," he said. "Sitting on your butt all day makes you fat."

"I'll remind you that you said that when you ask me for a raise," the captain growled. She looked at the trio. "Right, that means one of you stays here to help me. I guess it's Mora, since you other two are the computer experts."

Mora pouted. "I want to go with Tristan. Anyway, there's nothing much I can do to help you here, is there?"

"Yes." O'Connell was clearly not changing her mind. "We'll intercept with the ship in another hour, give or take. That leaves us only an hour and a quarter before it enters Earth's atmosphere. It's too close for comfort. What I'm going to have to do is attach the *Simón Bolívar* to the garbage ship and get ready. Tristan, you and Genia can have forty-five minutes to get aboard the ship and work on it. After that, I can't risk it. I'm going to fire my main engines and boost the bomb away from Earth. Then I'm going to overload the engines and detonate the *Simón Bolívar*. I can't risk it getting to Earth."

She didn't add that this would kill them all; she didn't need to, because they all knew it.

"Agreed," Tristan said. "If we can't stop it in that time, we probably never will. And — we understand. You do what you have to, Captain."

"Thanks for your permission," she said dryly. "Well, just an hour to the intercept. If any of you want to say your prayers, call anyone up, or just go somewhere and scream yourself hoarse, now is the time to do it. I want Tristan and Genia to join Brightman in the hold in thirty minutes. And Mora, you come here."

Tristan nodded and moved to the door. "I'll be there," he promised. He shot down to the room they'd been using, to where his desk-comp sat. After a moment's pause, he tapped in his parents' code.

The Screen lit up as the call was answered. His father stared back at him, blinking with surprise. "Tristan!" He sounded excited and worried at the same time. "Where are you? How are you? The shields don't have you under arrest, do they?"

"No, Dad," he answered. "We've cleared up that horrible mess."

"Thank goodness. Uh, here's your mother, too." He moved, allowing Mrs. Connor to join him.

"Tristan," she said, "are you coming home? You've heard the news about . . ." She couldn't bring herself to say *the end of the world*.

"I've heard," Tristan said. "But I can't come home,

I'm afraid. Um . . . Mora's with me." There was no time to explain the situation, and he didn't want to scare them by telling them what he was going to be doing. "Look, I just wanted you both to know that I love you."

"You're not angry that we didn't tell you that you are adopted?" his mother asked.

"Not anymore," he replied honestly. In fact, he'd hardly thought about that small problem for days. It was amazing how things fell into their true perspective when you weren't sure you'd be alive two hours from now. "I realize that I could never have had better parents. I've had . . . an example of how bad it can be." Poor Genia and that louse of a father of hers! "I just wanted to thank you for everything, and hope I'll see you real soon."

"Why can't you be here?" his father asked. "We kind of hoped we'd be together as a family, in case . . ." His voice trailed away.

"I'm kind of busy right now," Tristan said. "I'll tell you all about it when I see you, I promise." *If I ever see you again* . . . There were no guarantees. "Look, I've got to go. There are other people who have to call home. I'll see you as soon as I can, I promise." Before they could argue, he cut the call. There were tears welling in his eyes, and he tried to blink them away.

"That was kind of cute, in a sort of nauseating way,"

Genia said from the hatchway. Tristan looked around at her. "I'm glad to see that at least one of us has parents they actually like, though."

"They're nice people," Tristan informed her. "I'll introduce you to them when this is all over."

"Oh, yeah?" Nothing seemed to be changing Genia's attitude. "As what? *Hi, Mom and Dad, this is my friend Genia. She's a thief, out on parole from the Underworld. Make sure you count the silverware when she's gone.*"

"Why can't you just be nice to me for once?" Tristan asked her. "Instead of being sarcastic, or having an attitude? You'd be quite likable if you just tried."

"I don't *want* to try," Genia answered. "Look, I don't want nice relationships with people. I *know* what people are like. You can't trust them." She looked almost as if she were about to cry, which was something Tristan had never seen before. "My father? He abandoned me as a kid, and then tried to murder me because I got in his way. Shimoda? She promised to help me, but failed. My mom? She went and died, just when I needed her the most." She shook her head savagely. "I'm not about to trust *anybody*, brain boy."

Tristan felt horribly sorry for her. She was so lonely because she'd never found anyone to share her emotions, her needs, or her life with. "Not even me?" he asked her, praying she wouldn't simply laugh in his face.

"*Especially* not you, you jerk!" Genia yelled. "Because I think I *might* be able to trust you! And I don't want to. I'm only strong because I only believe in myself. I don't need you. I don't need anybody. I'm just putting up with you! You understand that?"

"Yes," Tristan said meekly. His insides hurt. He'd been hoping for more than that from her, but he supposed he should have known better.

"You don't understand *anything*!" Genia yelled. Abruptly, she grabbed hold of him, dragged him close, and kissed him.

Tristan almost panicked. He had been hoping she'd give him just a little encouragement, but hadn't really been expecting much. And now . . . he kissed her back, realizing he'd been wanting to do this for a long time. Then she pushed him away, and there really were tears in her eyes.

"Don't let this go to your head," she told him. "It's just that I'm panicking right now. I may die soon, and I just didn't want to die without kissing somebody, you understand? If we get through this, I'm sure my brains will come back to me again, and I'll kill you if you tell anyone."

Tristan nodded. He understood more than she probably knew. She *was* in a panic, but mostly because she was being forced to admit that she cared about somebody other than herself. Well, he'd deal with any problems later. Right now, he just felt kind of good about the whole thing.

"We'd better get down to the hold," he said gently. "We've got to learn what to do before we go across to the other ship."

"Right." Genia nodded, perhaps a bit too enthusiastically.

As he turned to lead the way from the room, he thought he saw a flash of motion in the corridor. Had Mora been watching them? Well, it didn't really matter. He and she were definitely through anyway. There was no way he could ever look at Mora again without remembering how she'd betrayed him. And then, later, wanted to kill him for what he had supposedly done to her. Mora simply couldn't accept that she was to blame for anything. But she was trying to make up for her mistakes, so Tristan wanted to give her that chance. But he knew he'd never feel any unique attraction again.

Besides, Genia would probably kill him if he so much as smiled at Mora the wrong way!

There was no other sign of movement until he and Genia reached the cargo bay. Brightman was already there, prepping three suits. He glanced up. "Ah, the innocents to the slaughter. Come in, guys, and start worrying. This is going to be hard on you both, and one mistake could kill you."

"Great," Genia muttered. "We're being escorted by the angel of doom." But there was a slight smile to the edge of her face, and her voice lacked its customary venom. Maybe she *was* in love, after all.

Tristan moved in and paid attention as Brightman explained all about the suiting up, checking and double-checking everything. It certainly was complicated. He glanced at the wall chrono. Ten minutes to rendezvous, and then . . .

"Right," Brightman finally said. "Enough talk, let's get suited. It's do-or-die time, kids."

Tristan could only pray it would be the former.

7

Shimoda and Van Dreelen strode back into the conference room at Computer Control. She was feeling a lot better than she had when she'd left, for several reasons. The most obvious was that they now had a chance at stopping Devon. The rest of the remaining board was there, waiting for them.

Therese Copin sniffed loudly. "I hardly think that this was a good time to go on a date," she commented.

"On the contrary," Van Dreelen said. "If the world is going to end, I'd sooner spend my time in the company of a beautiful woman than with a bunch of old complainers like you."

"However," Shimoda said, trying to ignore the compliment, "the world may *not* be ending. We have a chance. It may be a small one, but it's a chance." She informed them of Tristan's plan.

"It's a long shot," Jada objected.

"It's the only one we've got," Van Dreelen answered. "And Tristan has come through for us before. He's the one who stopped the Doomsday Virus. I have faith in him."

"In a fourteen-year-old boy and a self-confessed thief from the Underworld?" Miriam Rodriguez shook her head. "I can't believe we're stooping that low."

"It's not low," Shimoda answered, angry with these people. "They're both bright kids, with a lot more courage and resources than all of you put together."

Borden shifted in his seat uncomfortably. "We've been . . . discussing the situation since you left," he informed her.

"Oh?" She glanced sharply at their evasive looks. "And from the high level of cowardice in this room, I expect you've all decided to cave in to Devon's demands."

"It's better than dying!" Jada exclaimed. "Which is what you'd have us do."

"It is *not* better than dying," Shimoda snapped. "It's worse than dying, because you'd be condemning every living person on Earth to a potential living nightmare."

"Potential," Jada said, jumping on the word. "All right, even if Devon *did* want to cause mayhem and torture people, there's only a certain number he could hurt. The rest would be able to live as they are now."

Van Dreelen looked around the room. "I can't believe I've worked with you all these years and not seen before now what a bunch of creeps and morons you are," he said in disgust. "*Live as they are now*, indeed! You'd be condemning them to a lifetime of fear and uncertainty. And then, when Devon finally dies — or simply tires of his sport — he'd kill the whole lot of them anyway. And *that's* preferable to a quick death?"

"Haven't you seen the demonstrations?" Borden asked. "In person, outside, you *had* to have come through them. And we're getting so many on-line comments it's choking our system."

"Panicking, sheeplike masses," Van Dreelen growled. "You're listening to *them*? What about the millions who don't want us to give in?" He shook his head. "No, you're using their weakness to justify your own cowardice."

Shimoda took a deep breath, knowing what she was about to do would affect the lives of everyone on Earth. She tapped a button on her wrist-comp without being noticed. Tamra would know what the signal meant. "Are you all in agreement on this?" she asked. "Martin and

I think we can win, but we won't if you're all determined to surrender." She looked around the table. Almost everyone avoided her gaze, which answered her question.

"I'm with you," Anita Horesh said unexpectedly. "I'd sooner go down fighting than give in. But the three of us can't outvote the five of them."

"We don't have to." Shimoda glanced around as the door opened and a squad of shields marched in. "Ah, perfect timing." She gestured at the five board members. "These people have proven to be traitors. I want them confined to cells and isolated until I have time to press charges."

"Yes, ma'am," the captain agreed. He nodded to his men, who fanned out, their tazers conspicuous.

Borden paled. "You can't do this, Shimoda!"

"I can, and I have to," she replied icily. "If you don't have the courage to go through with this, step aside for those who do." She watched impassively as Borden, Copin, Rodriguez, Schein, and Jada were taken out, all protesting bitterly. When the door closed behind them, she collapsed into the nearest seat. "You realize that we've just done what we're trying to stop Devon from doing?" she asked Van Dreelen and Horesh. "We've taken over the world."

"The difference is," Van Dreelen replied, "that we're

trying to save it. And we'll give it back when we're done."

"I'll be lucky if all they do is fire me after this," Shimoda said. "But that will be a small price to pay if this works."

"We could just sit around and see what happens, but I prefer to be a man of action myself," he said, a mysterious grin on his face. "There's one more little secret I have up my sleeve, you know."

Shimoda glared at him. "This had better be the last," she warned him. "I don't date people who keep secrets from me."

"It's the last," he promised. "And I think you'll like this one. It's about Mars. . . ."

8

Jame struggled to get back the signal to Devon, but without success. As he'd feared, his clone was too smart to be caught by the same trick twice. But he couldn't simply give up trying. There had to be something he could do — there *had* to be!

The Administrator used a second comp to contact his colleagues on the *Santa Fe*. "Devon has decided to go rogue," he informed them. "And it looks as if your genius replacement for the boy is useless. I think it's time we stopped playing games and executed him as I intended all along. Your plan isn't working."

"Is that your solution to everything?" Anna Fried

asked after the time lapse for the signal to reach the ship. "Execute people?"

"They can't cause trouble once they're dead," the Administrator said coldly. "And I'm sure you want to come here to a pacified Mars, don't you? Well, that won't happen without a little spilled blood. I've tried what you wanted, and it's failed. Now I do it my way." He cut the link so there could be no more argument and turned back to face Jame. "Stop messing about there, boy," he ordered. "You've failed, and you're now completely expendable."

Jame swallowed, knowing that this time the man meant to kill him. He stood up, refusing to beg for his life. "You won't win," he promised. "You can't."

"I have." The Administrator signaled to the shields standing guard in the room. "Take him away and execute him," he ordered.

Jame started to think about running for his life, even though he knew he wouldn't get far without being cut down in a burst of tazer fire. Before he could move, however, the Screen lit up again, and a man whose face he didn't recognize seemed to look out at the scene in the room.

"This is Van Dreelen," the man said. "Shield code omega blue. *Now.*"

Two of the shields immediately whirled and fired on

their colleagues, cutting the men down in a hail of electrical tazer blasts. Jame was too stunned to move, as the two men then turned on him and the Administrator.

"It's over, Administrator," the captain said coldly. "Quietus was misinformed when they believed that we were all loyal to you. Some of us are loyal to Computer Control, after all. We were just waiting for the signal to strike, and it's arrived."

Jame stared at the man in astonishment. "You just pretended to be on their side?"

"That's right." The shield smiled tightly. "Mr. Van Dreelen knew this was coming, and had us pretend to defect so we could get inside the plan. Quietus is being broken up now, and we're taking control back. Our other men will be freeing the hostages, and Captain Montrose and his team. They'll be rearmed to join us."

"My men will fight you!" the Administrator vowed.

"I'm sure they will." The captain glared at him. "We'll take great pleasure in destroying all the sadists and traitors. And then in bringing you to justice."

"Then you've sealed your own deaths, too." The Administrator tapped his code into his wrist-comp. "I'm activating all of my bombs, and destroying the power plants." His face twisted as he sent the signal.

The shields both paled, and whipped their tazers into position. Only Jame remained calm. "No, you're not,"

79

he told the Administrator. "I changed their codes, and they're all harmless now. You were right, you should never have let me loose on the comp." He grinned at the shock and fury in the portly man's face. "It's all over, and you're going to be punished for what you've done. Personally, I think they should send you outside without a space suit."

"You haven't won yet," the Administrator swore. The captain nodded to his man, who took the Administrator by the arm. The Administrator shook him off, and tried to look dignified. "I can walk unaided," he said.

"Then walk," the shield snapped, gesturing with his tazer. They left the room.

Jame swallowed with relief and collapsed back into his seat. "This is incredible," he said.

"It's well planned," the captain answered. "Look, I have to get busy helping with the counterrevolution. You'll be safe; stay here. I'll have your family sent to join you. It's not going to be safe in the corridors for a while, as we capture the traitors." He nodded and left the room.

Jame was still astonished by what was happening. It was so hard to believe that it was all over. Only, of course, it wasn't over yet. He could hear the sounds of tazer fire in the distance, and knew that men and women were fighting and dying to free Mars once again.

Only this time there was a very good chance they'd succeed.

And there was still Earth to worry about. Jame reconnected to the Net, and started to try and track Devon again. This was no time to think only of himself and Mars; another planet was in peril, too.

The door hissed open, and a man staggered in. He was covered in blood, and there was a knife in his chest. Jame jumped in shock, and then recognized the man as the shield escorting the Administrator to jail.

"He had a knife," the man gasped. "Got away . . ." He collapsed to the floor, spraying a horrible amount of blood on the carpet.

Jame rushed to him. "Don't talk," he said, wishing he had some medical knowledge. He had already sent an emergency medical call from the desk-comp. "Help's on its way."

"He got away," the man repeated, ignoring Jame's advice. "Took hostages . . . your mother and sister."

"What?" Jame couldn't think. Just when he'd thought everything was safe, *this* happened! He tried not to imagine what might be happening to his mom and Fai right now. He knew that the Administrator would kill them if he felt threatened. Jame couldn't allow that to happen. He rushed back to the desk, and activated whatever security cameras were left.

It took him a couple of minutes to locate the three people, by which time a medical response team had come and taken the wounded shield away. Jame hardly noticed, so focused was he on his search. Then a camera near the docking bays caught the movement he was after.

The Administrator had a tazer, and an arm around Mrs. Wilson's throat. Jame's mother was clutching Fai to her chest frantically, obviously trying to protect the baby with her own body. She looked hysterical, which sent a stab of pain through Jame's heart.

"I won't let him hurt you," Jame vowed. "I promise." He bent to the controls, realizing that the Administrator was heading for his own ship. It was fueled and ready to launch. The monster had planned an escape all along, in case things went wrong. Well, Jame would stop that. He sealed the ship's docking clamps so that they wouldn't release. The Administrator wouldn't escape vengeance. But Jame had to get his mom and sister free. Only . . . how?

No tazers, because any shots would get his mom and sister, too. He needed something more subtle. . . . And then he had it. His fingers raced across the speedboard as they never had before. This was too urgent to make mistakes, so he focused intently. The airlock was the key. He alerted a shield patrol, having them send two men to the airlock to intercept the Administrator. He barely noticed that the fighting was slowing down. There were shield bodies all over the city, victims on both sides. But Montrose and his shields were winning the fight, and it couldn't last much longer. Jame worked quickly, praying he'd be done in time. And that he hadn't misjudged things. . . .

On the Screen, he saw the Administrator reach the airlock before the shields. Reaching around Mrs. Wilson, the stout man triggered the airlock door. As it opened, he urged his mom and Fai inside and joined them. There was a shout from the corridor as the two shields approached. The Administrator turned to face them, and, just for a second, the tazer was no longer pointing at his mother.

Jame tapped a signal.

The Administrator, his mom, and Fai all arched and yelled in pain before collapsing. Jame, his hands shaking, cut the electrical current he'd sent through the metal floor. It was enough to stun, but not to kill. He'd had no choice about hurting his family, but they were alive. He'd gladly accept whatever punishment his mom decided on later. At least he had saved their lives. Jame watched as the shields gingerly approached the airlock.

"It's safe now," he assured them. "And the Administrator's out cold. You can arrest him now. My mom and Fai just need rest, and they'll be okay."

The nearest shield glanced at the airlock comunit Jame was using. "Thanks, kid," she said. "We've got it now. Quick thinking."

"Yes," Jame said to himself as he cut the link. "Yes, it was."

He was still shaking as he sat back in the chair. Mars was free again, and Quietus stopped. His parents and Fai were safe, even if they'd be furious with him later. Everything here was over — he prayed.

But what about the rest of it?

9

Moss stood at the doorway as the last of the colonists filed into the assembly rooms. Then he nodded at the engineer on duty with him here. This was a scene being repeated in every city on the Moon. It was almost ten now, only two hours before the midnight deadline. The last possible minute. . . .

The doors hissed closed and sealed. The engineer then tapped the codes into the comp that shut down the fuel mix for the local reactor. There was a flicker from the lighting strips, and then they died entirely. A moment later the duller, orange-colored emergency lights came to life, bathing the room in a reddish glow.

It looked like ancient paintings of the Inferno, with too many people crammed into too small a space. Moss glanced at the engineer.

"Is it working?"

She checked her comp. "Well, the reactors didn't explode," she said, trying to sound cheerful. "That's a good first step. It means that Devon's little nasties won't be able to destroy the Moon, after all."

"No," Moss agreed. There was some relief in that announcement, but not enough. "Now all we have to do is hope we can survive the cure." He knew it was only his fear and imagination, but it was already starting to feel chilly in the room. Over the next two hours, it would *really* start to get bad. They had to hope they could dismantle the sabotage devices and restart the reactors in time to save their lives.

It was going to be a long two hours.

Already, people were murmuring. The pumps and heating elements that provided the normal backdrop of noise to life in Armstrong City were silent. It was unnatural here for silence to reign. Babies started to cry, missing the comfort of the humming. Moss knew how they felt. He almost wanted to cry himself.

Now it was simply a matter of waiting, hoping, and praying. There was nothing more that they could do. . . .

*   *   *

Jill Barnes had joined the shields originally because she wanted excitement. She'd grown up on a small autofarm out in Kansas, and it had seemed to be the dullest spot on Earth to her. She'd seen the glamorous life of a shield as a wonderful antidote to boredom.

Now she'd seen more action in the past couple of weeks than she'd wanted in a lifetime. How did that old saying go? *Be careful what you wish for — or it may come true.* . . . Well, she had literally asked for this. While she felt privileged to be trusted by Shimoda, she also felt as if she was being punished for her teenage wish.

The shield ship was hurtling through interplanetary space, in pursuit of the fleeing *Santa Fe*. Van Dreelen's codes had proven to be perfect, and the Quietus craft had shown up on their instruments immediately. The *Santa Fe* was a passenger ship, built for comfort and convenience. It wasn't meant to accelerate too fast, because that would upset the paying customers. This time, the flight consisted only of the Quietus rebels. There would be no innocent bystanders to worry about, thankfully.

The shield ship, on the other hand, was a much rougher craft, built for endurance and speed, not comfort. (*Especially not comfort*, Barnes decided as she shifted her backside again, trying not to have it bruised.) But they could outthrust the *Santa Fe* and were coming up on the traitor's ship now.

"Thirty minutes to intercept," Chen called out from the navigator's seat. He tapped the intercom to the rear cabin, where the assault crew was assembled. "Team to suits," he ordered. "Prepare for rendezvous." The plan was for Barnes, the pilot, and Chen to bring the shield craft in as close to the other ship as possible. Then space-suited shields would fire themselves across, and break through into the airlocks. Then they would take over the ship, arrest the Quietus members, and prepare for the return to Earth.

Assuming there was anyone on Earth left to return to.

Barnes was still worried, because all plans tended to have unexpected problems built into them. When you were dealing with people who would betray and plan to wipe out most human beings on Earth, there was no telling what they might do to try and save themselves. All she knew was that this wouldn't go as planned.

"Do you think there will be anything to return to?" the pilot asked her. He was a nice-looking young man. From his accent, she judged he was from one of the African states. He'd probably joined the shields for much the same reason she had, and was, by the look of his face, starting to regret it, too. "I mean, I have family back on Earth."

"We all do," Barnes told him. "They're doing everything they can to make sure we have a home to return to. But even if we don't, we still have to do our duty."

"And then what?" the pilot asked. "Don't get me wrong, I'm a hundred percent behind this. But what if Earth dies? Where do we go then? I heard the Moon has its own troubles, and that they might all be dead in a few hours. We can't go there. And Mars . . . well, who knows what's happening there?"

Chen glowered at the man. "We do what we must," he said. "And then we do what we can. We'll just have to see what happens. But you're right — these next few hours are critical. So let's do our part, shall we, and trust everyone else to do theirs."

"Yes, sir," the man agreed, bending back studiously to his controls.

Barnes couldn't help sympathizing with him, though. He'd only asked the question that had to be going through all of their minds.

What would be the fate of the human race after these next few hours? Who would survive — if anyone?

She shuddered. She had to put that question out of

her mind, knowing that she'd be unable to work otherwise. What she had to do was focus on her job.

The shield ship closed in. She could see the light from the *Santa Fe* with her unaided eye now. No running lights, of course — there was no need for them in space — but the lights from the observation deck windows. Cruise ships found that passengers simply loved looking out at the stars as much as possible, as well as at the planets and moons as they passed by. Barnes wished she had the time and the lack of urgency to allow her to enjoy the same luxury. But she didn't.

Chen cleared his throat. "Time to give our ex-comrades the bad news, I think," he decided. First he checked with the squad deck, and learned that they were suited and prepared for combat. Were there troops on board the *Santa Fe*? Barnes didn't know.

Chen tapped in a comchannel code to carry to the other ship. It wasn't answering on any frequencies to normal calls, of course, but Barnes knew they'd answer this one. She tapped the command to switch on all the shield ship's external lights. The *Santa Fe* could hardly miss the shield ship now, and they'd understand that their need for silence was long over.

"This is Computer Control to Quietus rebels," Chen said carefully. "There's no point in trying to hide from us any longer. As you can see, we're coming alongside your craft. You have two options: surrender now, or force us to attack and capture you." He paused, waiting to see if there would be any reply.

Barnes was rather surprised when the Screen came to life. Elinor Morgenstein, the old president of Computer Control, appeared in the picture. Barnes had never seen the woman before, of course — she had been far too important to meet with a lowly shield lieutenant — but everyone knew her face from the News-Nets. Now she looked older than her years.

"Chen?" Her lip curled. "They let you out of Ice, then?"

"I'm not one of you, and Van Dreelen knew it," Chen replied. "I was freed a while ago so I could help stomp your conspiracy. And this is the last part of the fight, Morgenstein. This is the bit where you go on Ice. Forever, I'm sure."

"I'm not going to prison," the woman answered haughtily. "None of us is. We didn't get this far simply to be thought of as foolish criminals who'd spend their last, futile years in a cell, dreaming of release and of what might have been. Surely you know us better than that, Chen."

"Yes," Chen agreed. "I'm sure you feel you're much too rich and noble to ever end up on Ice, like a common criminal. And I have to confess that you're all very uncommon criminals. But you're still criminals. And, like all crooks when they're caught, you're going to jail for the rest of your miserable lives."

"You don't even know that there will be an Earth to go back to," Morgenstein replied.

"No, we don't," Chen admitted. "But if there isn't, there will still be somewhere left where you and the others can rot. I aim to see that you end up there."

Morgenstein shook her head. "I'm almost sorry to disappoint you," she replied. "But we will not be going to jail."

"You can't escape," Chen warned her. "We're faster and better armed than you are."

"I know that," she answered. "But it all depends on your definition of escape, doesn't it?" She sighed. "Chen, I'm too old, too proud, and too rich to go to jail. We all feel that way. You are not taking us back; it's as simple as that." Her face softened. "But I will confess that you've won. Just don't be in any hurry to claim your prize." The comlink broke, and the screen went blank.

"What did she mean by that?" asked Barnes, puzzled.

Chen looked ashen. "I'm sure I know." To the pilot, he said, "Get us away from that ship — now!"

The man looked confused, but did as he was ordered. Barnes suddenly realized what Chen was driving at. She pulled a picture of the *Santa Fe* up on her screen. It was still glowing slightly from the escaping light.

Then the picture overloaded, washing out in whiteness.

"They blew themselves up," Barnes whispered as she watched the light dying down, and her eyes could start seeing things again. Debris was all that was left of the passenger ship now.

"They were too proud to go to jail," Chen said softly. "Well, it saves us the trouble and cost of a trial. They delivered judgment on themselves. I can't say I'll miss them."

"I was kind of hoping I'd get a chance to blacken their eyes," Barnes admitted. "I know it's not what a shield should do, but I wanted to just let them feel some of the pain they inflicted on all of us."

"Whatever afterlife you believe in, Lieutenant," Chen said gently, "I'm sure they're all being punished in it right now. Take what comfort you can from that." He tapped the comunit again. "Squad, you can desuit. The raid has become pointless. We're returning to Earth." He closed the unit. "And I just pray that there's something alive waiting for us when we get back," he said to Barnes.

"Amen to that," she agreed.

She glanced at the chrono. It was almost zero hour now. Before they could return to Earth, Judgment Day would have fallen. The human race would live or die in the next half hour. . . .

10

It was the most incredible experience of Genia's life — and she didn't have the time to enjoy it. She was outside the *Simón Bolívar*, holding on to a plastic rope and crossing to the old freighter. She was wearing a space suit, and there was nothing but that between her and the stars, billions and billions of miles away. She'd always thought that space suits were bulky, clumsy things, but the one she wore was actually quite comfortable and flexible, some kind of modern woven plastic. The helmet was much as she'd pictured it, with a screened visor through which she looked out at the universe. And there were two air tanks on her back, along with a temperature control unit that would keep her alive and fit.

There were the two ships and, beyond the freighter, the growing blue-white ball of Earth. If she looked over her shoulder, she could see the half globe of the Moon. But, around all of that, at immense distances, were the stars.

She wanted to float here forever, just soaking in the view. It was so astonishing, being in space like this, able to fall forever and never hit anything. The universe went on to unlimited horizons, and the thought humbled her.

But she had a job to do, and she was forced to ignore everything else. Holding on to the rope, she inched across the space between the two ships. Brightman had used a thruster pack to make the journey, and then set the rope up for her and Tristan to use. "A novice with a rocket in space equals trouble," he'd told them. "You do it the old-fashioned way." Actually, Genia enjoyed this; it gave her a few moments to simply look out at creation and feel the awe well up inside her soul.

By the time she reached the freighter, Brightman had checked for booby traps — as Tristan had said, "You have to expect the worst from Devon." Apparently, there weren't any, because the hatch was now open.

"No air inside," Brightman informed them. "It's an

96

automated ship, so there's absolutely no need for it. We'll have to work in our suits."

Genia winced. That would cause problems — even with these slim-designed suits, the gloves would make typing hard. And there would be no possibility of a verbal interface with the computer, so typing would have to do it.

There was no light, either, but Brightman had anticipated that, having brought along a couple of lamps that he set up in the control area. Genia looked around It was cramped, with only just enough room for her and Tristan to stand. At another time, she might have enjoyed being so close to him, but now she wished he'd take his elbows somewhere else. Brightman disappeared off to the engineering room, without any explanation.

Tristan hacked into the main computer, while Genia took the navigational one. "I'm going to try to access the command codes," he informed her. "You see if you can figure out how to change the course of this ship. If we can adjust the flight plan a little, we can make it miss Earth."

"Yes, I can just about work that bit of logic out," she told him sarcastically. While she had to admit that she was a lot fonder of him than she'd ever imagined she would be, that didn't mean he would be getting away with anything with her. He'd have to take the rough with the smooth, that was all.

As she worked, she couldn't help seeing Tristan — or feeling him, if either of them moved more than an inch or two. She had rather surprised herself when she'd kissed him. She hadn't actually planned it — at least, not consciously — but it had just seemed like the thing to do at the time. She thought about all of her objections to him. He was way too stiff and noble, for one thing. And without much sense of humor. He took himself and everything else so seriously. He was rich, and she was pretty much poor. He was from Above and she was from the Underworld. They only had two things in common, really: their skills with computers and a desire to save the world.

On the other hand . . . well, he was cute, he was considerate, and even if he was a bit of a self-righteous pain, he did mean well, and he was doing his best to save the human race. How could you *not* like a guy like that?

What would come of this, she didn't know. She wasn't exactly the sort of girl he could proudly introduce to his parents or friends. She was better off, since she had no friends, and only one parent — who could rot for all she cared.

All of these thoughts would be pointless unless she

could get the controls working. "How's it going?" she asked him.

"Not well," he confessed. "Devon's triple-encoded this — at the very least. Maybe more. It's going to take a while to get through." He sighed. "I wish I could take these gloves off; they're slowing me down."

"Tell me about it," she muttered. She bent back to her task, and took a sip of water from the straw near her mouth. Her throat had gone dry when she looked at the chrono.

They had eighteen minutes left — and Captain O'Connell had threatened to start work on blowing the ship up when they got down to fifteen. . . .

She focused on the comp. Devon had encoded this one, too, even though he hadn't expected anyone to access it. Secrecy and security seemed to be as natural to him as breathing. And he had a devious mind, so none of her usual patterns of search was working here. Instead, she had to guess, flying blind along logic pathways. Her head hurt as she focused.

"How's it going, guys?" the captain asked a minute or so later over their headsets. Her voice sounded tense, as well it might, considering what she was planning.

"Could be better," Genia said.

"It's slow work," Tristan added.

"That's what I was afraid of," O'Connell replied. "Well, it's time for plan B. You may as well give up now."

"I'm staying," Tristan said firmly. "The extra minutes might be all we need. And if we're going to die, we may as well die here as over there."

"Do what you have to, but I've never given up in my life," Genia agreed. "And since there's so little of it left now, I don't see any need to develop new habits."

The captain sighed. "I figured you'd say that," she admitted. "Okay, try to fasten yourselves down. I've attached the *Simón Bolívar* to your ship. I'm going to start boosting, and see if we can deflect its path. Brightman, get back over here. I'm going to need help."

"'Course you do, Captain," his voice came in. "I never did figure out how you got anything at all done without me around. Is this the wrong time to ask for a raise, if I'm so invaluable?"

"Ask me again in twenty minutes. Now move it."

Genia wedged her feet under a small rail running around the base of the floor. It had probably been fastened there for just such a reason. Repair crews sometimes had to board these scows in space for emergency fixes. Now she should be okay when the thrust came.

It came a moment later, a gentle push to one side

that made her rock a moment before regaining her balance.

Wait a minute! *Emergency fixes . .*

There had to be a way for an emergency repair crew to log in to the computer and download whatever was stored in its memory to help them work. Feverishly, she ignored her assigned task and started scrolling down the options until she found what she was looking for. With a howl of pleasure, she started the repair file going.

"What are you doing?" Tristan demanded. "I'm locked out!"

"Relax, brain boy," she told him. "It's the diagnostics. I'm running the program for self-repair."

"That won't do anything," Tristan complained. "It's not broken."

"No," she said patiently, "but it will give us the access codes when it's done, because it thinks we're the repair crew. We just have to wait."

"It's a very old machine," he complained. "And we don't have very long before we blow up. How long will the routine take?"

"How should I know?" she snapped. "I didn't see you having any better ideas."

"No, you're right," Tristan admitted. "I didn't." There

was a short pause. "Whether it works or not, it's a clever idea."

"Yeah, that's me all over." She grimaced. "And if this thing goes boom, it *will* be me all over."

"I don't want you to die," Tristan said gently.

"Trust me, *I* don't want me to die, either." She smiled. "But I know what you mean. Thanks. I just wish they had some way you could kiss somebody else in a space suit."

Tristan chuckled. "Maybe you should design a system, when you've got the time."

"Don't think I can't, brain boy." She glanced at the computer, which was still running the diagnostic. Then she looked at the chrono. Eight minutes . . .

"Response is really sluggish," O'Connell reported in. "But I don't dare strain the ties by applying any more thrust. And I can't let us get any closer to Earth, guys. I'm sorry, but I'm going to have to set us off."

"We understand," Tristan said quietly. "We can't risk Earth."

O'Connell made an odd sound. "It was nice knowing you guys. For teenagers, you weren't such a bad lot. Right, here we go. . . ."

Genia felt giddy and sick. She was going to die now. Maybe for a good cause, but she'd never really wanted to die for *any* cause. Especially not now, when she'd decided that she wanted Tristan after all. There were so many reasons to live.

She remembered the sight of the blue-white ball of Earth. And one very good reason indeed to die . . .

"Hold it!" Tristan snapped. "We've got the codes!"

Genia opened her eyes and stared at the computer, blinking with the answers they needed. Hope suddenly surged through her entire body, like a jolt of electricity. She felt as if she'd been tazered. "Yes! I did it!"

"Are you certain?" asked O'Connell breathlessly. Genia could hear the strain and hope in the captain's voice.

"Yes," Tristan said. He and Genia had been typing furiously at their boards, which had both suddenly opened up. "We've got control of the ship now."

"I'm altering the thrusters," Genia reported. "Matching your thrust and velocity. You should start seeing a real change in heading now."

"I am indeed!" O'Connell said, excitement and relief stark in her voice. "Guys, I'm going to kiss you both when you get back here. And buy you the best meal on Earth when we're home again."

"Well, we're not home yet," Tristan pointed out. "And Genia would probably punch your lights out if you kissed me."

"One kiss I might allow," Genia said, grinning. "How are we doing?"

"Beautifully," came Brightman's answer. "We're definitely going to miss Earth; it's safe, guys."

"Right," O'Connell said. "If you can keep the ship on that heading and thrust, we'll be fine. I can start to disconnect the *Simón Bolívar* now."

"Great," Tristan answered. "I'm locking in the program so that Devon can't do what we just did and regain control."

"It wouldn't matter if he did," Brightman informed them. "I planted a little bomb of my own in the hold. As soon as the freighter's far enough away from Earth, I aim to detonate it. He's not getting this sucker back."

"Don't be too hasty with that trigger," Genia warned him. "I've only just survived one near-death experience. I don't want to repeat that again. My stomach wouldn't take it."

"Relax, kid," he assured her. "I want the two of you safely back here before we do anything like that."

"Okay," Tristan said, pushing back from his panel. "I think I'm done here. The controls are locked. How about you, Genia?"

"Perfect, as ever. I've set the thrusters to use up every last atom of fuel. It should send the ship way off the normal flight paths. If we detonate it in about an hour, it won't affect anything."

"You're wonderful."

"Yeah. I know it. I'm just glad that you appreciate me, too."

O'Connell's voice broke in again. "God, it's getting way too smug for my liking over there. The two of you had better get back here on the double. I may have to deflate your egos to be able to fit you back in the *Simón Bolívar*."

Genia laughed, and turned to go. Tristan collected both lamps before following her. It figured: The guy was terminally tidy. She took one lamp from him and stowed it on her belt.

In the hatchway, she paused just a moment. The plastic rope stretched some five hundred feet now, back to where the *Simón Bolívar* floated. Beyond it was the globe of Earth, surrounded by the eternal stars.

"Isn't that just the most beautiful sight you've ever seen?" she asked Tristan.

"If I say yes, will you punch me because I didn't say you were?" he asked her.

"Just this once, no," she promised with a grin. "Okay, enough gawking. Let's get back before our ride leaves."

Together, they pulled themselves along the rope, back to the ship. Genia hated that last step, back into the metal world beyond, out of the universe again. But

105

she forced herself to make it. The hatch closed behind them, and Brightman started the air pumps. As soon as he gave the word, Genia cracked her helmet, and removed it. Tristan grabbed her and kissed her, and she just enjoyed the feeling for a moment, before pushing him away.

"Give you a little encouragement," she grumbled, "and look at you. We've still got work to do, you know."

He didn't look bothered. "I guess you're just addictive."

"Yeah, I am that." She finished taking off her suit. She had her street clothes on under it, minus her boots, which she'd left in the cabin. Barefoot, she padded along the corridor toward the bridge. "Let's go see the fireworks, shall we?"

The three of them returned to the control deck, where O'Connell greeted them with the promised kiss — thankfully, on the cheeks. "Great job, guys," she said happily. "I am *so* glad we survived this one, along with the rest of Earth."

"Yeah, it is exciting," Genia agreed. She looked at Mora. "I'm even almost glad to see your face again, too."

"Don't work too hard at being nice," Mora replied stiffly. "It doesn't suit you."

It figured that she'd be the only one not happy to see

Genia back. Well, tough She could survive Mora's dis-
like. "Are we putting distance between us and that float-
ing bomb?" she asked O'Connell.

"Darned right we are," the captain answered. "I'm
going to chance it for another five minutes, then we detonate her."

"I think we're all in favor of that," Tristan agreed.
Then he blinked. "What's that?"

Everyone followed his gaze. On the Screen, a third
ship was suddenly registering. Genia could have sworn
it hadn't been there a moment ago.

"Visitors?" O'Connell suggested.

"No," Tristan said, his voice suddenly sounding very
tense. "There's only one person that could be. It's
Devon — he's been hiding, waiting to watch Earth die.
And now he's coming after us . . ."

Genia stared at the approaching craft. This would be
her first meeting with Tristan's clone. And she had an
ominous feeling that Devon intended it to be the final
one . . .

11

ristan closed his eyes and winced. It was all too logical, of course: Devon loved to watch, so he'd accompanied his bomb, hoping he'd be able to watch the end of all life on Earth. Now, however, Earth was saved, and Devon was bound to be really mad about it. "Can we outrun that ship?" he asked Captain O'Connell.

She gave him an incredulous look. "We're not built for speed," she pointed out. "And that ship is a shield craft. It *is* built for speed. We wouldn't stand a chance." She chewed her lower lip. "Besides, it's almost certain to be armed."

"Great." Would Devon just come alongside and then

blow them up? Tristan didn't think so — it wasn't in-your-face enough for Devon's style. "And we're totally unarmed."

O'Connell shook her head. "I wouldn't exactly say that," she replied. "In fact, I've got a couple of tazers on the ship. Just in case." Seeing Tristan's incredulous look, she explained, "Well, you know, things get pretty rough in some of the spacers' bars, so we like to have a little . . . insurance."

"Well," Genia said sarcastically, "which of us is going to sit in the airlock and take potshots at that ship?"

"I think the captain's got the right idea," Tristan said. "Devon's not going to blow us apart from a distance. He likes to see things happen. And he's probably really annoyed with us right now for ruining his scheme. I imagine there's a good chance he'll want to come over and yell at us first."

Mora was incredulous. "Why would he do that?"

"Because I aim to provoke him," Tristan explained simply. He glanced at the captain. "But he's going to expect trouble, I'm sure. I can't have one of those tazers, because he's bound to be watching me. And he's going to suspect you and Mr. Brightman, because you're adults."

"Which, by process of elimination, leaves the dimwit and me," Genia said. "That sounds reasonable."

O'Connell went to a small locker and pulled out the two weapons, which she tossed to Genia. "You know how to use those?"

"Oh, yes," Genia answered. "I've had a bad childhood. I know all kinds of stuff I'm not supposed to." She checked one gun and slipped it into the back of her pants' waistband, where it wouldn't be obvious from the front. Then she looked at Mora. "I don't imagine you know one end of this from the other, princess, so I'll explain. This is the safety." She clicked it over. "You just point and pull the trigger." She clicked it back, and handed it to Mora. "Just remember to switch it over if you have to use it, okay?"

"I think I can manage that," Mora answered stiffly. She followed Genia's lead in hiding the weapon.

O'Connell and Brightman were busy at the controls. "Maybe I should blow the bomb now," Brightman suggested, his hand over the radio trigger.

"Not yet," Tristan replied. "We're still kind of close."

"Devon might try and kill us all," O'Connell pointed out. "If he manages, then he can regain control of the bomb again. I don't think we want that."

"True enough," Tristan agreed. "But I'd like the chance to detonate it later, if we can. The farther away it is from Earth and us, the better."

Brightman considered. "Okay, I'll set it on a count-

110

down — thirty minutes. The only way to stop it will be to detonate it earlier than that. But in thirty minutes, no matter what any of us does, it'll blow." He grinned. "Even you two geniuses couldn't stop this one — it doesn't have a computer, just an old-fashioned chrono fuse."

"That sounds perfect," Tristan agreed. "In fact, it might provide us with a distraction. Can you set the main comp Screen to follow the path of the ship? The explosion might distract Devon and give us a chance to jump him, if it should be needed."

O'Connell nodded her approval. "You've got a devious mind, kid. I think I'm getting to like you." She bent to the task.

Genia moved closer to Tristan. He liked it, but there was no time now to enjoy her company. "You think he's really going to come over here?"

"I can virtually guarantee it," Tristan assured her, praying he was understanding his clone correctly. "He's going to have to confront us; that's the way his mind works. He has to *win* at all costs."

"He's not at all like you, then, except in that," Genia said quietly. "You never give in, either. Do you?"

"I can't," Tristan explained. "This is too important. I can't let him kill us." He managed a weak smile. "We haven't even been on a date yet."

"Ah!" Genia grinned back. "Now I'm encouragement for your flashes of inspiration, eh? I like that."

"But you're wrong, you know," Tristan couldn't help adding. "I *am* quite like Devon. And that terrifies me."

Genia frowned. "You're nothing like him!"

"We're *clones!*" Tristan exclaimed. "We have virtually the same makeup in our minds and bodies. And both Devon and the other clone, Jame, are criminals. I must have a leaning that way myself, and that scares me. What if I give in, like they did?"

Genia shrugged. "We'd make a great team of thieves?" she suggested. "Come on, Tristan — you'd *never* give yourself over to the dark side. You're *way* too moral for that."

"I wish I could believe you," he said miserably.

Brightman glanced up from his panel. "Talk about timing. The bomb's started the countdown, and we're getting an incoming call from you know who."

"Let's talk," O'Connell decided, and they all glanced at the main Screen when Brightman brought up the image.

It was, as they had expected, Devon. Tristan could never get over the shock of how much they looked alike, even down to their hairstyle. Only the clothing they wore was different.

"Somehow," Devon said, his lip curling in anger, "I just knew it had to be you. Connor, you're a jerk, setting yourself up to be killed like this."

Tristan forced himself to appear calm, even though his heart was racing. He *had* to be able to manipulate Devon now. . . .

"So you're going to kill me?" he asked. "Big deal. It doesn't matter. I've *beaten* you, you idiot, and *everybody* knows it. I destroyed your Doomsday Virus, and now I've stopped your Armageddon bomb." He shrugged. "So, you can kill me. But you can't *win*."

Devon's face twisted in fury. "You haven't won!" he yelled. "I can destroy you! That means *I* win!"

Genia snorted. "Doesn't look that way to me, moron." She glanced at Tristan. "And you were afraid you might turn into a spoiled brat like this? Somebody who can only cry over his broken toys and lost dreams? You could never sink so low."

Good girl! Tristan thought. She was really punching Devon's buttons. His clone was looking absolutely livid.

"Go ahead," Tristan jeered. "Blow us up. Big deal — you still lose, and everybody on Earth knows I've beaten you."

"You're really asking to die, you know that?" Devon growled. Then his eyes narrowed. "Wait a minute! You

113

are asking to die, aren't you? Why?" He glowered at them suspiciously. "What are you up to? What don't you want me to know?"

Brightman couldn't help but glance at the ticking chrono on the panel, and then flushed as he realized what he'd done. Tristan could barely keep from grinning — it was so perfect!

"You've fixed my bomb ship to blow up!" Devon realized. "*That's* why you want me to destroy you — so I can't take control of it again!" He shook his head. "No way is that going to happen. You're going to die, all right — but not by being blown up." The picture died.

O'Connell glanced up from her instruments. "He's moving in to rendezvous with us," she reported. "It looks like you read him right, Tristan."

"Thanks to Mr. Brightman," Tristan said. "I was going to dare him to come over and deal with me man-to-man, but that was much better. Devon simply can't resist coming over now."

"And we'll be ready for him," Genia promised, taking out her tazer.

"Not yet," Tristan warned her. "Devon may have something else planned. We have to know he's not set any more traps yet before we spring our own."

With a sigh, Genia put her weapon away. "Okay. But I

really want to inflict some serious pain on this guy, okay?"

"No argument from me."

The ship shuddered as Devon's stolen shield ship docked. There was a metallic clang as the airlocks joined and then opened.

"Get ready," Tristan said. Actually, he was the most tense person in the room because he'd finally be meeting his murderous clone face-to-face. He wasn't sure how this would go, but he had to somehow make certain they all survived the meeting.

Then something popped into the room, and exploded. Not exactly exploded, but it felt like that. Tristan was stunned into immobility, frozen where he stood, barely able even to breathe. A grinning Devon followed the blast, which seemed to have affected everyone else in the room, too. He was carrying a tazer of his own, and he swiftly frisked Tristan, then Brightman, and finally O'Connell. He lingered a bit over the captain, and by the time he started to move on Genia, Tristan discovered that he was able to start moving again.

"Uh-uh," Devon cautioned him, gesturing with the tazer. "I can see that the concussion grenade is wearing off. Great armament on that shield ship, eh?" But he kept half an eye on Tristan as he quickly frisked

Genia, missing the tazer in her back completely. He was just as fast and inefficient with Mora, trying to divide his attention. Then he moved back to the doorway. "Isn't this cozy?" he jeered. "Sort of like shooting fish in a barrel."

Seeing him this close was even more shocking than seeing him on a Screen. Tristan stared at him, and shook his head. "How can you look so much like me," he asked, "and be so different?"

"Because I'm smarter than you," Devon replied. "I'm the one who'll live through this meeting." He grinned wider. "Actually, I'm kind of glad that I'll be killing you in person. You've been such a pain to me, ruining my plans. I will be so glad to see the last of you."

"You've not been very good at killing him yet," Genia jeered. "He's escaped every trap you've set for him, and he'll escape this one."

"Oh, yes, the street rat." Devon looked her over with contempt. "How you've lived this long is beyond me, but it ends here and now."

"It'll take a better man than you to kill me," Genia sneered. "You talk big, but underneath it all, you're just a boy playing with toys. You are way out of your league."

"Say what you like," Devon replied calmly. "I've still won, and I'm going to kill the lot of you. But first, turn off that bomb."

"No," Brightman said.

Devon gestured with his tazer. "Do it, or I shoot you."

Brightman laughed. "You're going to shoot me anyway," he pointed out. "You're going to have to come up with a better reason than that."

"Very well," Devon agreed. "Whoever helps me, lives. Whoever doesn't, dies. Anyone here want to live, or should I just shoot you all now?"

Tristan moved slightly to the side, away from Genia. He had to give her a chance to get Devon, and that meant drawing his clone's attention to himself. The problem was, that could get him killed really fast. "What's up?" he mocked. "Don't tell me that this life-destroying bomb of yours was your last idea? Can't think of any new ones? Is that why you need it so badly?"

"I'll think of new ones if I need to," Devon snapped. "But this one isn't finished yet. Who'll stop the countdown and live?"

"How can we trust you?" Tristan asked him. "You're not very good at keeping your word. You'll kill anyone who helps you anyway."

"If they're on my side, they'll live," Devon promised. He gestured with the tazer. "Stop moving, or I shoot you now."

"Go ahead," Tristan said. "And you'll know I've

117

beaten you. How will *you* live with *that*? The knowledge that you were always second best?"

"I'm not second best!" Devon yelled. He whipped the tazer up, poised to fire. Tristan was staring at his own death, as the maniac's fingers hovered over the trigger. "I'm better than you, and I'll prove it." His finger tightened.

Genia moved faster than Tristan could follow. Her tazer was out and fired before anyone could move. The tazer in Devon's hand glowed slightly as the blast hit it. Devon screamed and dropped the gun, clattering, to the floor. He stood there, yowling, rubbing his hand.

"Boy, *that* was fun," Genia remarked. "I've been wanting to hurt you for the longest time. Just give me a reason to shoot you again, please!"

Tristan breathed a huge sigh of relief, realizing that they had finally won. Genia had come through when most needed, as he had been sure she would. "Nice going," he complimented her, picking up the fallen weapon and placing it beside the captain. "But there's no need to shoot him again. We just need to imprison him and take him back to Earth for trial."

"I don't think so," Mora said firmly from behind them. Tristan looked around to see that she had her own tazer pointed at them. "Okay, dumbo — drop the gun before

I shoot you. And don't think I won't, either. I'm just itching for the chance to hurt you."

Genia hesitated, and then dropped her tazer to her feet."And what are you doing, no-brain?" she asked.

"I'm taking Devon up on his offer," Mora said cheerily. "I'm switching sides."

Tristan stared at her in horror. How could she do this?

It was the ultimate betrayal.

12

Genia glanced at Tristan.

"I *told* you not to trust her," she said. "That girl is simply not stable."

"*This girl* has a gun on you," Mora warned, moving around them to join Devon, who was watching what was happening with interest. "You little witch, I've been dying to get rid of you for the longest time. Worming your way into Tristan's affections and stealing my boyfriend!"

Genia snorted. "I think you've got it all backward — which is no surprise. *You* betrayed *him*, remember? And dumped him. I didn't do anything until you'd already thrown him away." She grinned. "And it really burns you up that I got him, doesn't it? You *should* join up with Devon — two losers together."

"Two losers?" Mora shook her head. "From where I stand, we're the winners. We'll be alive, and you won't be. Besides, I have a plan."

"Wow," Genia said in mock astonishment. "There's a novelty! You with an idea! And what's this plan of yours?"

"I'm going to get Devon a new identity." Mora gestured at Tristan with her tazer. "As you. He'll be the hero of the day, and able to do what he likes. And with me there to tell everyone he's the real Tristan, who would ever suspect the truth?"

Devon's face lit up at the thought. "Hey, I like that idea! Maybe you have your uses. What's your name again?"

"Mora," she growled, obviously annoyed that he hadn't remembered.

"Right, yes." Devon nodded. "You made *such* a cute couple before she came and stole Tristan away. But now, *we* can be the cute couple. That should be fun."

Tristan swallowed. It was a scary thought — Devon taking his place, pretending to be him . . . and being able to work unsuspected, trusted even . . . He could rework the Doomsday Virus and take over Earth. "Then

I guess you don't need the bomb anymore," Tristan commented.

"Maybe, maybe not," Devon replied. "It might be nice to have it in reserve. Just in case plan A doesn't work out."

Mora actually looked a little worried at the thought. "You don't need to destroy Earth," she said. "You can just rule it, with my help."

"Why should you care what I do?" asked Devon, puzzled.

"My parents and sister are down there," Mora said. "I don't want them hurt."

This obviously made little sense to Devon. "You care about them?" He shrugged. "Well, we could bring them with us, I guess. Though why you want them is beyond me."

Genia laughed. "Gee, doesn't he sound like a prize catch?" she mocked. "Is he worth trading in the human race for? Is he really your type?"

"He can be," Mora insisted. She appealed to Devon. "You do find me attractive, don't you?"

"Attractive?" Devon was confused, obviously not having thought about the matter. "Uh, yeah, I guess you are kind of cute."

"How romantic," Genia gloated. Tristan didn't see why she was provoking Mora so hard — there was very little preventing Mora from gunning her down. "I'll bet he doesn't kiss as well as Tristan."

"Kiss?" Devon looked repulsed. "You don't think I'd *touch* her, do you?"

Mora looked shocked, and Genia laughed even louder.

"There you go, beautiful," she jeered. "He won't even touch you. Even *he* thinks you're sick. And you want to be his honey?" She laughed and laughed at the thought.

"Shut up!" Mora screamed. She brought up her tazer, and fired it. Tristan had seen this coming, and threw himself in the line of fire to save Genia. He expected to feel electronic fire burning him up, but instead felt only the deck as he hit it, hard, forcing the breath from his body.

Genia grabbed up her own tazer again. "That was sweet," she said to Tristan as he winced and tried to sit up. "But not really necessary. You see, I never did trust her, so I told her the wrong way of setting the safety. She's got it on, not off." She leveled the tazer. "Now, drop it, because *mine* is switched on."

Mora's face was twisted in fury and bitterness, but she did as she was told. "Now what?" she asked coldly. "Are you going to kill me?"

"No." Genia helped Tristan to his feet and handed

him her weapon. "But I am going to do something I've wanted to do for the longest time." She whipped around and her right fist connected hard with Mora's jaw. The other girl slammed backward into the bulkhead, then slipped unconscious to the floor.

Gena rubbed her fist. "Boy, that *hurt*," she complained. "But it was very, very satisfying." She glanced at Tristan. "I don't know what you ever saw in her. You've got lousy taste in girlfriends."

"Including you?" Tristan asked. He was still a little shocked by Mora's betrayal.

"Especially me." Genia grinned. "I'm the sort of girl your momma always warned you to watch out for."

"I'll watch out for you," Tristan promised. "It'll be fun."

"This is so nauseating," Devon commented. He didn't seem at all bothered by what had happened. "Don't tell me you enjoy trading spit with girls like this?"

"Trust you to not get it," Tristan commented. "Well, you'll get something — life on Ice, if I'm not mistaken. Or maybe they'll bring back the death penalty, just for you."

"I don't think so," Devon answered. "You're as big a jerk as ever, you know that? I won't be sorry to see the last of you."

"I think you're missing something here, dodo," Genia said. "We're the ones with the gun, and not you."

"And I'm the one with the brains, not you," Devon replied. His hand flickered out, and another of the concussion grenades exploded.

Tristan couldn't move again, but Devon obviously had some sort of an antidote, because he could. He whirled around and left the room. "I've changed my mind," he called. "I *am* going to blow you out of space, after all." Tristan struggled to move, but couldn't. He heard his clone running down the corridor, and then the clang of the airlock before his frozen limbs finally unstuck. He started forward, but O'Connell yelled, "No!"

There was the sound of Devon's ship disengaging, and Tristan realized any pursuit was futile now. "No!" he yelled in frustration. "Once he gets away from us, he'll just open fire. We can't fight that."

"Don't be so sure of that," the captain grunted. "I *hate* being concussed, and he's going to pay for that."

"Our ship isn't armed," Genia pointed out. "And tazers won't do anything at this range." She sounded really scared now, obviously at the end of her own inventiveness.

"No, but bombs will." Brightman was adjusting his controls. "We've still got control over his other ship, don't forget. I'm bringing it back around. All we need is a few more minutes. . . ."

"If he'll give them to us," Tristan muttered. But at least there was hope. "Uh . . . aren't we kind of close to the thing if you blow it up?"

"Yeah," the engineer agreed. "But we're a lot closer to his weapons, so I think we'll just have to take that chance, don't you?"

"I'm all for it," Genia assured him. She grabbed hold of Tristan's hand. "I think we'd better sit this one out."

"It's bound to get rough," O'Connell warned them. "Strap yourselves in."

"Right." Genia moved to the closest seat, and started to attach the webbing. Tristan went to where Mora lay. "Don't worry about her," Genia complained.

"I can't help it," he answered, lifting her unconscious body and slipping it into a seat. It was difficult fastening the web, since Mora kept falling over. But Genia pointedly didn't help. Tristan could hardly blame her. Once he was done, he strapped himself in, and used the closest comp to call up an image of what Devon was up to.

The shield ship had moved off, and was paralleling them in space. As Tristan watched, several hatchways began to slide open in the ship's side. "Uh, guys," he called. "I think you'd better hurry. He's getting ready to atomize us." His throat felt tight. He reached out and squeezed Genia's hand, and she squeezed back. He wasn't sure which of them was comforting the other.

The shield ship rolled slightly, bringing its firepower to bear on the *Simón Bolívar*. It was only a matter of seconds now till the cannons were charged and ready to destroy them. Sweat trickled down Tristan's back, and his palms were very moist. So were Genia's, though her face showed none of the fear she had to be feeling. She met his eyes.

"You've got a lousy idea for dating, brain boy," she complained. "Next time, *I* pick the party, okay?"

"I promise," he answered, trying to smile.

It was time to die. . . .

And then a bright light filled the main Screen as the bomb ship detonated. There was nothing like a shock-wave, of course, since there was nothing to conduct one in the vacuum of space. But there was debris. Some of it came toward them. . . .

. . . And ripped into Devon's ship, which was between them and the bomb. The shrapnel and metallic fragments tore the shield ship apart. O'Connell had the *Simón Bolívar*'s thrusters at maximum now, and Tristan was slammed back in his seat by the acceleration. He managed to keep his Screen focused on the shield ship, however, and watched in awe as the metal debris sliced through Devon's craft. Great rips and tears opened up in the ship, and he could see air venting into space.

Then something must have struck the ship's drive, because there was a second blinding flash. Tristan's eyes were blinded by the burst of light, and he couldn't see anything for dozens of seconds. There was a rattling on the shell of the *Simón Bolívar*, however, and several larger, louder thumps.

"Just minor debris!" O'Connell yelled above the sound of the thrusters. "We'll be fine."

"This would make a great VR program," Genia grunted. "For masochists." She glanced at Tristan. "I've got bruises in places you definitely don't get to see."

"But we're alive," Tristan pointed out with growing elation. "We survived it!"

The ship shuddered again, and he hoped he was right. Then his eyes cleared, and he could see once more. On the Screen, all that was left of Devon's ship was a thinning field of junk.

It was all over, but Tristan had a curiously empty feeling. Devon was dead, and he had lost a clone. A very evil one, to be sure, but it felt as if some part of him had died.

"I think," O'Connell said, "that we'd better take the

three of you back to Earth, before you cause me any more trouble. I may not survive another hour with you guys."

"Yeah," Genia said with a wide grin. "We're real trouble, aren't we?"

13

Moss was finding it harder and harder to move, even though he forced himself to do so. It was the only way he could retain even the slightest bit of warmth. He looked around the room at the rest of Armstrong City's population. Most parents had wrapped their children in whatever spare blankets there were, in a futile attempt to keep them warm. But there was nothing any of them could do about the growing staleness of the air.

It had been the hardest, longest, coldest two hours of his life. There were already four people with frozen fingers who would need emergency medical treatment, and Moss thought they were lucky that nobody had died yet. But it was only a matter of time.

The chief engineer moved slowly toward him. "Midnight," the man said through chattering teeth. "The devices should all have triggered now. And, if we're right, they won't have any effect."

"To be honest," Moss said, "I think I'd be relieved to die right now. It would have to be better than this."

"Not much longer," the man answered. Moss realized that he still didn't know the man's name. He'd have to remember to ask later. "There haven't been any explosions that I can detect." His fingers could hardly work the keys on his wrist-comp. "It looks like our plan worked."

"Part one of it," corrected Moss. "You stopped us from being blown up. Now can you stop us from freezing to death?"

"Working on it, sir," the engineer replied. His stiff fingers tapped out the codes. "That was the restart signal," he explained. "There will be a short delay, to be absolutely certain that Devon's devices have all triggered and won't cause problems. Then the reactors should come back on line."

"How long before they start purifying the air and bringing up the heat?"

"About thirty minutes," the man answered. "And I know — we may not all survive that long."

He was right; two of the people died as the minutes dragged on. Moss wasn't sure if any of them would last, to be honest. The terrible chill seemed to have settled into his bones. Every movement hurt. Many people had given up struggling, and were simply sitting with their families, huddled together. Moss wished he could be with his own, but he felt it was important to be seen not giving up. That was the problem with being a public figure: You couldn't always do what you wanted, and had to do what was expected of you instead.

Eventually, there was a slight breeze. Moss thought he was imagining it, but then there came a second one, this time very definite.

The air was coming back!

He turned to the chief engineer, who studied his wrist-comp and nodded. "Power's restored," he reported. He looked as if he wanted to smile, but was afraid his face would crack under the strain if he tried. "Heat's edging up a bit, too. We made it."

"Yes," Moss agreed, looking at his people. With the slow movement of air, many were starting to stir, realizing that their ordeal was actually coming to an end. "We made it."

Life would go on.

*   *   *

Tristan's legs were very unsteady as he clambered out of the *Simón Bolívar* and into the docking bay at Schwarzenegger Space Port. "You don't know how glad I am to be back on the ground," he said, wanting to get on his knees and kiss it. "And for the ground to not be radioactive."

"Yes, I do," Genia told him. "I feel exactly the same way." Then she glanced across the bay. "Uh-oh. Welcoming committee. I hope."

Tristan followed her gaze, and saw Shimoda and Van Dreelen striding toward them, followed by several shields. For one terrible second he wondered if Shimoda had lied to them, and they were actually being placed under arrest again. Then he saw the smiles on her and Van Dreelen's faces, and felt ashamed of himself for not trusting them.

"Thank God you're safe," Shimoda said, with obvious emotion. To Genia's discomfort, the shield grabbed the girl and hugged her tightly. "I was so afraid for you."

"Yeah, break a couple of ribs, why don't you?" Genia grumbled. But there was a smile on her face, too, and she hugged Shimoda back. Van Dreelen shook Tristan's hand.

"There aren't words," the man said simply. "You both saved Earth."

"Save some praise for us," O'Connell complained, coming down the steps and zipping up her jacket. "And we aim to bill you for this trip," she added with a smile. "We never did get our run completed."

"Whatever you charge, we'll pay," Van Dreelen promised. "With a hefty bonus."

Brightman grinned. "Then I think this calls for a celebration, Captain," he said. "And it's definitely the right time for me to ask for a raise."

O'Connell stopped beside Genia and Tristan. "Nice going, guys," she said. "Any time you want another ride into space, ask someone else, okay?"

"Trust me, I'm staying on the good Earth for a long time now," Tristan assured her with feeling. "I've had enough of space to last me a lifetime."

The captain smirked. "It gets into your blood, though. You'll be back." She tossed them a lazy salute. "Catch you around." Then she and Brightman ambled off together.

"Mora?" asked Shimoda.

"In the ship," Tristan said, a strange lump in his throat. "Unconscious."

Shimoda nodded to the shields, who went aboard to collect her. She looked at Genia. "You must pack quite a punch."

"It had a lot of emotion behind it," Genia answered.

"What will happen to her?" Tristan asked nervously. "I mean, I know she has to be punished, but . . ." His voice trailed off under Genia's glare.

"She's being sent for correction," Shimoda said gently. "There's obviously something wrong in her head. She needs treatment more than punishment."

"Says who?" argued Genia. "I'm all in favor of punishing her for the rest of her life."

"You're a little prejudiced," Tristan informed her.

"No, I'm not," Genia objected. "I'm a *lot* prejudiced. She betrayed you twice, which is bad enough. But she betrayed me once, which is even worse. I don't aim to let her get a second try."

"She won't get one, I promise," Shimoda answered. "And, this time, I have the power to make that promise hold. At least for now." She exchanged a glance with Van Dreelen.

"Well, everything's finished then?" Tristan asked. "We can go back to normal now?"

"I don't think we can ever go back to what we once thought of as normal," Van Dreelen informed him. "There are too many changes that have to be made. Quietus and Devon showed us that our society is very vulnerable, and we have to patch it up considerably."

"Or," Shimoda corrected, "change it considerably. But that's for a future discussion. Right now, there's

135

one last little thing to clear up, and we thought you might like to be with us on this, Tristan, since it relates to you."

Puzzled, Tristan nodded. "I thought we'd cleared it all up," he said. "Devon's dead, and so are most of the Quietus traitors. The Moon's okay, and Mars is getting back to normal. What have I forgotten?"

"Just one thing," Shimoda said with a mysterious smile. She and Van Dreelen led the way to a shield hovercraft, loaded with armed shields in riot gear. There was also an elderly-looking woman with a scowl on her face. "This is Dr. Emili Dancer," Shimoda said, introducing Tristan and Genia.

As the craft got under way, Dr. Dancer studied Tristan with a frown. "You're one of the clones?" she asked sharply.

"Yes, ma'am," Tristan agreed meekly. "Devon is dead."

"Hmmm . . ." The doctor examined him from where she sat. "You don't look that special to me. Well, I'm sure I'll get a chance to check you out fully later."

"He's not a laboratory specimen," Shimoda objected.

"You mind your business, and I'll mind mine," Dr. Dancer answered. "But you're right; nobody should be allowed to do damage like this on the human race."

"Where are we going?" Genia demanded, obviously unable to rein in her curiosity any longer. "If somebody doesn't tell me, I'm going to get very annoyed. And ask Tristan — he'll tell you that you don't want to know me when I'm annoyed."

"Trust her on that," Tristan agreed. He, too, wanted to know.

Shimoda explained. "Dr. Dancer has found the lab where they cloned you, Tristan. We're going in to arrest the people responsible, and to shut them down."

"Wow," said Genia sarcastically, "we're taking you back to your cradle, Tris. Should be a hoot and a half."

Tristan was kind of numb. They had found where he, Devon, and Jame had been created. What would he see there? Would he learn anything about himself?

The trip wasn't far, and at Dr. Dancer's direction, the shield ship dropped down beside a skyscraper. "Basement level," the old woman snapped. Shimoda gestured, and the shields went into action.

They were astonishingly efficient. They went in through the door, and within half a minute, Shimoda received an "all clear" from their leader. The shield officer brought the rest of them inside. There were agents all over, escorting men and women in smocks and suits into the entrance, electronically shackled.

"We've attached their comps," one shield reported.

"We're downloading all of their data. It looks like they've been pretty busy over the years."

Shimoda glanced at the worried prisoners. "Take them away," she said in disgust. "Lock them up. I'm tempted to suggest forgetting that they're there, but I suppose they deserve a trial."

The shields nodded, and started to clear the building. Dr. Dancer bent over one of the comps, and tapped up a schematic of the place. "This way," she said brusquely, and set off down a corridor. Tristan, Genia, Shimoda, and Van Dreelen fell in behind her. For an old lady, she certainly moved very spryly.

They came to a large locked door, and Dr. Dancer scowled. "Code locked," she grunted.

"No problem," Genia assured her. The girl moved forward and started to work. It took her thirty seconds, then the door sighed open.

"Come on," Dr. Dancer said. She led the way into the room. Tristan didn't know what she was doing, but he was consumed with curiosity. Inside the room were twelve containers. Four were open, and eight were still sealed. Machinery hummed, maintaining them. They were about four feet tall and cylindrical.

"What are they?" Tristan asked, curiously.

The doctor gestured at the open ones. "Your cradles," she said. Then she pointed to the locked ones. "Your brothers."

Tristan was stunned. "My *brothers*?"

"Eight more of the clones," Dr. Dancer said. "They wanted to be certain they had viable fetuses. They're the backups, in case anything went wrong. They're viable."

"What do you mean?" Genia asked.

"She means," Van Dreelen explained, "that there are eight more just like Tristan still in there, as babies, waiting to be grown." He grinned at Tristan's confusion. "It looks like your family has just increased by a whole lot."

"Eight more of me?" Tristan gasped.

"Better than eight more Devons," Shimoda replied. "We can't leave them here, so they'll have to be raised. It looks like you're going to be big brother to a bunch of geniuses."

Tristan didn't know what to say. Eight more like him . . . It was incredible.

The future was going to be . . . definitely weird . . .

Later, they were all back in Computer Control. Tristan was quite impressed with the place, built over several acres in New Jersey. The conference room had seats for twenty-four, but there weren't that many people present now. Dr. Dancer had disappeared, to see to the hatching and care of the other clones. Tristan was starting to look forward to seeing them grow. His folks wouldn't be able to adopt them all, of course, but Tristan had been promised he could be a part of their lives as they grew, and that would be terrific.

Shimoda sat in one chair. Beside her was her secretary, Tamra. Next was a man who had been introduced as Peter Chen, and a Lt. Barnes, a nice-looking, cheerful shield officer. Then came Van Dreelen, and another woman, Anita Horesh. There were several shields present. Finally, there was Tristan and then Genia, both feeling very uncomfortable and out of place in this room of power.

The main door opened, and five more people marched in. They didn't look at all happy as they took the remaining seats. According to the desk-comp, they were Luther Schein, Miriam Rodriguez, Dennis Borden, Badni Jada, and Therese Copin, the final members of Computer Control's board. Shimoda had explained that she'd had them locked up earlier, and they all looked majorly annoyed with her.

"I trust you've all been brought up to date?" asked Van Dreelen.

"We have," Borden said crossly. "It seems that you

had more luck than you deserved, and managed to save Earth after all."

"You might look a little happier about it," Shimoda said. Tristan was impressed. He'd had the chance to talk to her, and he really liked her. She'd told him how intimidated she'd been by these people, but you wouldn't know it now. She was telling them off, and they deserved it. The five of them looked a little cowed.

"We are happy," Copin insisted. "But we're also annoyed that you took it on yourself to act without us."

"Because you wouldn't act," Van Dreelen said smoothly. "But, at this moment, only those of us in this room know that. As far as the general public is concerned, you're all as much heroes as we are. They believe that you were behind our plans one hundred percent. And they need never know the truth."

Borden scowled. "Why do I have the feeling that you're about to blackmail us?"

"Because I am," Van Dreelen answered, smiling. "We will allow your reputations to remain intact; nobody will know that you actually wanted to turn Earth over to that lunatic, Devon. But the price is your resignation from the board. We clearly can't trust you with power again."

"You can tell people that the strain was too much, and you need privacy and quiet," Shimoda suggested.

Borden glared at them. "And if we don't, you'll tell the truth," he said. "And we'll become despised pariahs."

Shimoda shrugged. "That's about the size of it, yes."

Borden nodded. "You have my resignation," he said. "I'm getting too old for this anyway." One by one the others agreed with him.

"Wonderful," Van Dreelen said. "You will, of course, all get full pensions. And retirement homes as far away from here as we can arrange."

"And you'll replace us with your flunkies, no doubt," Schein complained. "So you'll stay in charge of the world."

"That's the last thing I want," Shimoda assured him. "Frankly, I'll be glad to get out of Security's seat now that Mr. Chen is back."

"And I was always in favor of a divergence of opinion," Van Dreelen added. "We'll be bringing in some new boards members who'll argue with us, trust me. We have no desire to be emperor or empress of Earth. Good-bye," he added, pointedly.

The five ex-board members filed silently from the room, and Van Dreelen breathed a sigh of relief. "Thank goodness that's over. I was horribly afraid that they'd kick up a stink."

"They're politicians," Chen pointed out. "They know how to change with the times. They're just glad to get out so generously, I think. So — who *are* you going to replace them with?"

"Well," Van Dreelen said, "I'm now technically the president, since everyone above me is gone. So . . ." He moved to the president's seat. "Next order of business," he told Tamra, who was recording. "Miss Shimoda is removed as head of Security, and Mr. Chen is returned to his old post. Pay and privileges to be backdated, of course, to take in the time he was on Ice."

"Thank goodness for that," Shimoda said, in evident relief. "You're welcome to it back. I've grown heartily sick of it. I'll be *so* glad to get back to being a captain again."

"Whatever gave you the idea you were going to be a captain again?" asked Van Dreelen harshly. "We've already promoted Lieutenant Barnes to your old job."

Shimoda looked startled. "But I thought . . ." Her voice trailed off, and a very suspicious look crept over her face. "What are you doing to me?" she demanded.

"New head of Planning," Van Dreelen answered, and Chen nodded. He was obviously in on this. "You've proven that you're absolutely marvelous at forward thinking, and we need you on the board."

"Oh, no!" said Shimoda firmly. "No, I just want to go back to being a shield."

"Sorry, you're overruled," Chen said. "And your job's been filled, remember?"

143

"We need you, Taki," Van Dreelen said, suddenly serious. "This whole mess has shown us how vulnerable Computer Control is. We need to make it a lot safer. And you're the best person to head the changes." He glanced at Tristan and Genia. "You'll need a good staff, of course, and I've got two good suggestions. Tristan is obvious, and Genia has managed to break into most of our systems. She'd be perfect to make sure they become foolproof."

"Me?" Tristan squeaked. "Work for you?"

"Seems like a great idea to me," agreed Shimoda slowly. "If I'm being forced into this, at least I'll have a good staff."

Genia snorted in amusement. "Me? Work for the establishment? You've got to be dreaming, folks. No way! I'm happy doing just what I am — being a pain for the lot of you. Don't worry, though — I'll keep on doing my best to break into your systems, so you'll be able to tell how well you're doing."

Tristan looked at her in confusion. "But . . . if I'm working for Computer Control . . ." he said. "Am I going to be dating you or trying to arrest you?"

Genia shrugged. "You'll have to figure that one out for yourself, brain boy. You wouldn't want a nice, simple, uncomplicated life, would you? 'Cause you sure aren't going to get one." She looked very pleased with

144

herself. Tristan could see that she was right: His life was *never* going to be dull.

"So," Tamra said, "is that about it for now? I've started drawing up a list of possible appointees to the rest of the posts."

"Good work," Van Dreelen said. "I hope your name is on the short list for head of Personnel. You seem to have a knack for it." He looked at Tristan. "There's just one last thing," he said. "After all you've been through, I thought there was somebody you ought to say hello to." He nodded at Tamra, who activated the wall Screen.

A familiar face looked out at him and, for a second, Tristan thought it was Devon. Then he saw the red desert out of the window behind the boy's face and realized this had to be his other clone sibling, Jame, on Mars.

"Hi, Tristan," the boy said. "Glad to see you. Well, I *will* see you in a few minutes, when your signal gets to me here. I heard about what you did, and I'm really proud of you. It would be terrific if we could meet up sometime. I didn't know until recently that I even had a brother."

"Hi, Jame," Tristan said, really pleased to see that this other clone of his hadn't turned out to be bad, after all. "I heard what you did, too, how you saved Mars.

145

Nice going. And I think it would be a great idea to get together. And we'll have eight kid brothers soon, too."

The Screen suddenly split, and another face, identical to Tristan's and Jame's, appeared. "A family reunion?" the youth asked. "And you didn't invite me?"

"Devon?" It was a shocked chorus from around the table.

"Yeah." Devon grinned. "Surprised to see me, huh? When will you learn that I'm smarter than you thought?" Genia dived for the deskcomp, but Devon clucked his tongue. "You won't find me," he promised. "I'm hidden in a place where none of you will *ever* find me. I just wanted to let you know that you'd better never let your guard down. Because I will be back." He grinned. "See you, brothers!" He vanished from the Screen.

Tristan sat there, struck dumb. It was impossible.

"We saw his ship blow up!" Genia protested. "He's dead!"

"He doesn't seem to think so," Van Dreelen said dryly. "We'd better start a search for him, I guess."

"He may not actually be alive," Tristan said, when his brain kicked in again. "That was just a message, and a pretty general one at that. He didn't exactly respond to us. He just said generic things."

"What do you mean?" asked Shimoda.

"It might just be a very sophisticated computer pro-

146

gram," Tristan explained. "One last joke that Devon left for us. He might not be alive at all — but wants to scare us into thinking he is."

Van Dreelen blinked. "Well . . . which is it? Is he dead or alive?"

"I don't know," Tristan admitted. "We'll just have to wait and see. . . ."

THE END
?

about the author

JOHN PEEL is the author of numerous best-selling novels for young adults. There are six books in his amazing Diadem series: *Book of Names, Book of Signs, Book of Magic, Book of Thunder, Book of Earth,* and *Book of Nightmares.* He is also the author of the classic fantasy novel *The Secret of Dragonhome,* as well as installments in the Star Trek, Are You Afraid of the Dark?, and The Outer Limits series.

Mr. Peel currently lives just outside the New York Net, and will be 145 years old in the year 2099.